SKIN WALKERS
LETO

By
Susan A. Bliler

www.susanbliler.com

ACKNOWLEDGMENTS
Cover Artwork done by:
Cindy Hubbard

Cover fonts, spine, and back cover done by:
Cindy Hubbard

This story is a work of fiction. Names, characters, places, and incidences are either products of the author's imagination or used fictitiously. Any resemblance to actual events, locales, or persons, living or dead, is entirely coincidental.

DEDICATION

DJ

Thank you for always being there brother

Illegitimi non carborundum

Chapter 1

Shy swallowed hard. Her wet fingers trembled as they reached up for the doorknob. A second loud explosion rocked the lab and had her fearful hands latching onto the doorknob and turning frantically.

She'd been held captive at Megalya Labs for what she guessed had been about five months. A former intern, she'd been sickened when she discovered that the so-called scientists were experimenting on live human specimens.

Confronting Dr. Chambers had been the biggest mistake of her life. When she'd threatened to call the authorities and have the lab shut down, he'd had her hauled from the lab. At first she thought she was being escorted from the building. She'd fought and cursed the other technicians for allowing Dr. Chambers to abuse the handsome man she'd seen strapped to the table in the glass partitioned exam room. She wasn't so lucky. Instead of being ejected from the lab, she was dragged to her own exam room where she'd been beaten, stripped, and examined against her will, and that had only been the beginning of her hell.

At twenty-six, she was just finishing her final semester of college. As part of the requirement to earn her degree in Cellular Biology, it was mandatory to complete a ten-week internship with one of the dozen or so medical facilities and labs that existed in the North West region. Foolishly, she'd chosen the Megalya facility because it boasted some of the most renowned Biomedical Scientists of the generation. She knew from research that their work was far more advanced than that of the other labs…if she'd only known then just exactly how advanced! Her intention was to use the internship experience to help get her into graduate school. Now, she didn't want to ever see another fucking lab for as long as she lived, even if it was only a few more moments!

A loud crash sounded overhead. The cement walls of the small exam room she was kept in fractured. Huge cracks opened up on two of the walls and zigzagged up and across the ceiling. She blinked and sputtered as debris rained down on her upturned face. *God, please don't cave in, please don't cave in, please don't cave in!*

Her eyes darted to the sink in the corner that had been shooting water into the air since the initial explosion had shaken her from her sleep. The water on the ground was slowly rising and she wasn't sure if she was more terrified of drowning or of being crushed by the thick concrete ceiling.

Turning she gripped the doorknob with both hands and attempted to open it. Five months of being underfed, abused, kept in the dark, and experimented on had left her weak. *Too weak!* A whimper escaped her lips as the overhead lighting blinked out for a few fleeting seconds. The alarms that had been screeching for the past ten minutes ceased momentarily then shrieked back to life when the lights flashed back on.

"HELP!" Shy screamed as she banged on the door. She didn't want to die here away from her family. Her thoughts flashed to her sister and a dull ache settled in her chest.

She'd wondered over the past five months that she'd been held captive what her family had been told. Had they even been told anything? If left to her imagination, her poor mother probably thought she'd been murdered and buried in the woods. Now knowing what she did of the Megalya technicians, Shy was certain they'd formulated some elaborate lie and fed it to her family. Her parents would take it at face value, but her sister would be an entirely different story.

Just as Shy would if the situation were reversed, she knew her sister would search to the ends of the earth to uncover the truth. The two talked daily…hell almost hourly and there was no way Shy would disappear without first talking to her sister. It had been so long though that Shy wondered if they all thought she was dead.

The thought of her sister mourning her death sparked Shy to scream louder and bang harder on the door. "HELP! LET ME OUT! I'M IN HERE! SOMEBODYYYY!

The sound of gunfire had her clamping her mouth shut. She pressed her ear to the thick iron door and strained to listen harder. Just on the other side of the door she could hear muffled voices. With her ear still to the door, she was thrown back with the wind whooshing out of her lungs as the door was kicked in.

Pain throbbed in her chest and jaw but were a secondary concern as her lungs struggled to take in air. Her eyes took in the dark clad form that filled the doorway as she used her arms and legs to scramble away from the menacing figure. As the large man entered, black smoke billowed around him and poured into the room. Shy moved faster to get away. When her back hit the wall, she could only watch as a second person appeared. Both wore full black fatigues and had their faces covered with dark masks. Dark glasses hid any view of their eyes. They looked like some military Special Forces team, and the automatic weapons each man held left Shy wondering if she should be relieved or terrified.

"Walker?" One of the men asked in a gruff tone. She couldn't tell which one spoke though because the masks covered their mouths.

How do they know about Walkers?

"Can't scent her. Too much smoke." The man closest to her bent and grabbed her wrists, hauling a startled Shy to her feet before lifting her into his arms. "Better safe than sorry." He motioned toward the other man with his head, "Find Conn. Let him know we have a female prisoner. Tell him to send Aries."

Terror was instant. *Prisoner?* Unsure whether they meant that they knew she was being held against her will or whether they meant she was now *their* prisoner Shy screeched, "Wait!" She tried to push out of the man's hold, but had little strength to do more than place her hands on his chest. "Wh-where are you taking me?"

He turned his face towards hers, but his covered features gave no hint at emotion. "Stay calm. We're getting you out of here."

Still unsure of whether he was a "good guy" or a "bad guy", Shy stammered, "Wh-who are you?"

He was already carrying her effortlessly out the door when he responded simply by saying, "Walker."

"Walker? Is that your name?"

The man stalled and turned to stare at her. Shy only saw her own reflection in his dark glasses and cringed at the sight of herself. Her cell hadn't had a mirror, only a metal frame cot with a flimsy wanna-be mattress, one small sink and metal toilette.

Shy couldn't take her eyes off her reflection, she looked different. Too thin, too pale, too haggard. Her once glossy, fiery, red hair was now dull and lifeless. Even her once vibrant blue eyes now seemed dull and flat. Her self assessment quickly ended when the stranger leaned forward and sniffed at her loudly for several minutes before finally pulling back. He began walking again, this time much faster.

"Wait!" Too much excitement and adrenaline left her wiped. She rested her head against the guy's chest. "Th-there's another prisoner." She didn't want to forget about the captive that had caused her own incarceration.

"Don't worry; my Commander's got your mate."

Shy tried to lift her head and failed, able only to gape at the man. "My what?"

"Mate. My Commander has freed him. He's safe, you don't need to worry."

"He's not…" she didn't get to finish the sentence. Another loud explosion rocked the facility. The man holding her crushed her head into his chest and took off at a dead run. She couldn't see anything but heard a loud crash just behind them.

The man holding her yelled, "Shit! It's coming down!"

Shy kept her eyes tightly closed and curled one fist into the man's thick military-style vest as she silently prayed, *Please not like this! I don't want it to end like this!*

Breathing became difficult and she realized that dust and smoke filled the air. The man holding her continued to run with her as if she weighed nothing. The loud moan of metal twisting could be heard and everything was silent for one eerie moment before the ground shook and an ear shattering crash rattled her teeth. Shy held her breath and knew she was dead. A few heart pounding moments later she felt the blistering cold of a Canadian winter's night freeze her still wet skin. Her eyes flew open and the first thing she saw was the breath she held escape her lips on a cloudy sob of relief.

It was dark, and more fatigue-clad figures raced toward them.

"She's unharmed," the man holding her spoke. "She's the other one's angel. Where's Aries?"

Someone approached. "They have the male captive in the chopper, he put up a fight." The other man who spoke laughed, "He thought Conn was Megalya. Aries is tending to Conn."

Conn? Shy remembered the name, it was rare. The logs at the Megalya facility had detailed records on an individual named Conn whom they believed was one of the elusive Skin Walkers.

The man holding Shy growled.

"It's alright York. Conn's fine, it's just a bloody nose, but you know how Aries overreacts whenever he gets even a scratch."

York? Shy lifted her head to stare at the young man standing in front of them. Her gaze met that of a young man with soft brown eyes. She stared at him as the adrenaline wore off and she began shaking uncontrollably.

"Shit bro, she's soaked. You better get her onboard before she freezes to death."

She was pulled tighter into York's chest as he stalked toward a waiting helicopter. "James, tell Conn we'll follow in the BlackBird."

The young man smiled over at them, "Okay. I'm riding with Conn and Aries in the Raven." His smiled broadened, "I wanna be there when her mate wakes up." He beamed at Shy, "Your Walker's a bad ass. I haven't seen anyone give Conn such a run for his money since the time Aries called him on."

These people thought the male she'd attempted to rescue was a Walker! She hadn't believed that anyone outside of the Megalya was aware of the supposed existence of Walkers. She wanted to ask the young man how he knew what a Walker was but he sprinted into the darkness; besides her teeth were chattering so badly she doubted she'd be able to formulate a coherent sentence.

York tucked her head closer to his chest and took off at a run. She felt him lunge and she could feel the weightlessness of being airborne before the sound of feet slamming on metal registered. He released the hold on her head and she looked up to discover they were in the cabin of a military-style helicopter.

"Aries coming?"

Shy scanned the cabin and was unsettled to discover three other soldiers crammed along the bench opposite them.

"No," York responded loudly over the sound of the blades as they whipped to life. "Let's move!"

"Yes Sir!"

Even though she couldn't see their eyes, Shy could feel the men assessing her. When one leaned forward she couldn't help but flinch as she clung to York. Seeming to notice, the man backed up a fraction. "Sir." He held a blanket out and York quickly unfolded it and draped it over her.

"I need more."

Three more blankets were thrust toward them and York used them all to cover her up, even lifting her slightly to tuck part underneath her. Wearing only a flimsy hospital gown, the garment was soaked and afforded little protection against the chilly night.

Freezing and terrified, Shy still didn't know whether or not these were the good guys or the bad guys. She did know, all too well, the type of treatment she endured at the hands of the Megalya technicians, and one thing was for certain, they wouldn't give a damn if she was comfortable let alone froze her ass off. Still, she had to know. "Wh-where are you taking me?"

The chopper was so loud she didn't think York heard her, but after a few moments he dropped his head and removed his glasses before pulling down the black mask that covered the lower portion of his face. He had sea green eyes set in a pale face with a striking red goatee covering his upper lip and chin. He was handsome. "We're taking you to safety. You'll be with your mate. The Megalya won't hurt you again."

Relief washed over her and she couldn't help the tears that flooded her eyes and spilled onto her cheeks. Their confusion over her relationship with the other prisoner would need to be addressed, but right now she didn't care what they thought as long as York spoke the truth. Her fingers ached from being fisted in his protective vest, but for some reason she refused to let go, too afraid it was a dream and she'd wake up back in her cell.

York pulled her closer and rubbed her back in a gesture of comfort.

"Son of a bitch!"

She peeked up and realized the words were spoken to York through a headset he had covering one ear.

"What is it?" he growled.

"We're leaking fuel York. Took a hit coming in." There was a pause, "We won't make it to Montana."

"FUCK!" York slammed his head back against the metal of the helicopter's cabin.

The voice in his ear piece spoke again, "Conn said he'd circle back."

York's tone was clipped, "How far ahead is he?"

The pilot responded after another brief minute of silence, "Far enough that if he comes back they'll need to refuel."

York dropped his eyes to Shy and his gaze narrowed on her. She simply blinked back up at him wondering what this meant for her safety. "Tell him to stay his course. We'll find shelter, repair the BlackBird, refuel, and depart ASAP."

The helicopter banked sharply to the right and Shy squeaked in fear as she clamped her eyes closed and lifted her arm higher to wrap around the back of York's neck.

"EASY!" he barked and Shy's eyes slammed open as she released her hold afraid she had upset the large man.

"Sorry Sir," the pilot spoke then continued in a regretful tone, "York? The Raven's turned and is circling back. Conn refuses to arrive with the Walker and not his angel. I've got orders to set down within a mile of the nearest town. Looks like we're headed to Lethbridge."

Shy felt a rumble deep in the man's chest then he was barking orders. "Get out of uniform boys. Marko, get to town and secure us six rooms. The rest of you secure the perimeter. Contact me through the mist if there are problems."

Peeking over her shoulder Shy caught a glimpse of the three men stripping out of their military gear. Quickly she buried her face back in York's chest and kept it there until she was blasted with cold air when the door to the helicopter slid open. Looking up, she saw a dark haired man move to the ledge of the helicopter and her heart skipped a beat. He wasn't wearing a parachute and was too close to the edge for her comfort. When he jumped from the still moving chopper Shy sat up and screamed.

Chapter 2

"Jesus Christ!" York grabbed her shoulders and spun her to face him, "What's wrong?"

Shy was hysterical. "H-he jumped without a chute!"

The other two men who'd stilled at Shy's scream looked from her to York with worried gazes. York's frown deepened and he motioned with his head for the two men to exit the cabin. Both jumped without chutes and York cursed under his breath as Shy paled visibly. He placed her on the bench beside him and stood to close the cabin door before reclaiming his seat. When he reached for Shy she recoiled further into the corner and dropped her gaze.

"What's your name?" he asked loudly. When she didn't answer he shouted, "WHAT. IS. YOUR. NAME?"

"Sh-Shy."

"Listen Shy, my men had military chutes that are designed to not be noticed," he lied. "We're Special Ops. We're trained to go places and do things that appear to be impossible. My men are safe." She looked at him with uncertainty but he noticed her deep frown seemed to ease by a fraction. He reached toward her again but ignored her flinch as he clicked a seat belt around her waist.

"ETA Tito?"

"Soon's your men give you the all-clear you can relay to me and I'll find us a spot."

Shy heard York cursing under his breath and could've sworn she heard him say, "Damn humans. We need a Walker pilot."

York frowned at her, "How long have you been mated to the other captive?"

Shy shook her head. She was about to tell him that she was mated to no one, but a rapid beeping blared to life and a red light attached to the ceiling of the helicopters cabin began blinking wildly.

"Goddamn it!" York growled. "Put her down Tito!"

"I'm trying!" The words were shouted.

York buckled a seat belt around his lean hips then reached for Shy. He unfastened her belt and yanked her into the wall of his chest, his arms wrapping around her like two steel bands to lock her in place.

"This might get bumpy," he whispered at her ear.

From the ear piece she heard Tito's shouted, "HANG ON!"

The rear end of the helicopter whipped around and the chopper banked sharply one direction before jerking violently in the opposite. Shy squealed and latched on to York's vest, burying her face against his chest.

"I've got it, I've got, I've..." there was a hard bump that jarred Shy's bones and a loud slow whirr sounded before Tito finished, "GOT IT!"

The loud whomp, whomp, whomp of the helicopter's blades slowed and then finally stopped. Shy was still clutching York's vest when his hold on her loosened. "You alright Shy?"

She simply nodded without looking up.

York reached between their bodies and unfastened his seat belt. Then he was standing and taking Shy with him, bundle of blankets and all.

Outside of the helicopter it was still just as dark and just as cold as it had been forty minutes earlier when Shy had first been rescued. A short dark skinned man circled the helicopter and asked, "Any word?"

"Where are we?" York countered.

The small man, who Shy assumed was the pilot Tito responded, "About two clicks east of our designated LZ.

Shy looked up in time to catch York focusing his gaze on something in the distance. She followed the path of his eyes afraid he'd seen something or someone. Instead she was greeted with dark woods, covered with a fine layer of Canadian snow. When she looked back up at York he was still intently focused on something and stayed that way for long minutes before he finally blinked and answered, "It's clear. Marko's securing rooms; Bodi and Lok have just secured transport and will be en route. ETA, five minutes." He turned from Tito and stalked toward the woods with Shy. "Secure the site. I'm hiding Shy in the woods in case anyone saw us go down. We still don't know if the Megalya are following."

Unintentionally whimpering at the thought, the sound provoked a hard look from York. "Don't worry Shy. You belong to one of us, which means it is our honor to die defending you. If the Megalya come, they'll have to kill me to get to you."

She knew the revelation was meant to be comforting, but it wasn't. She didn't want the Megalya chasing them and she sure as hell didn't want this gentle giant dying over her. Guilt gnawed at her as she watched Tito over York's shoulder. The small man pulled a firearm from a holster at his hip and hunkered down beside the helicopter to scan the area.

York carried her away from the chopper and into the woods. It got darker the further they got from the clearing and it wasn't lost on her that she was being taken into the woods by a stranger that just happened to be some special forces assassin and was built like a brick shit house.

"Y-you don't have to carry me. I can walk." If he was going to kill her in the forest, she at least wanted a running chance.

York didn't even look at her. "You have no shoes."

She opted for a more direct route, "You could let me go. I-I haven't done anything wrong." Tears flooded her eyes, "I just want to go home."

York kept walking. "You are safe. I thought I told you this. We'll take you to your ma…" He didn't finish the sentence, instead frowned at her before averting his eyes. It was silent before he emitted a low growl.

Shy drew in a deep breath. She was fading fast. As usual, she was starving. They weren't fed often in the Megalya cells and after months of going without nourishment, her body had begun breaking itself down to find nutrients. She was exhausted from the rescue and the emotional roller coaster she'd been on for the past few hours. She wanted to laugh at how ludicrous the situation was. She was alone in the forest with a stranger who had just growled at her and she was too damn tired and weak to care.

Letting her head fall against his shoulder she felt his body tense before he inhaled deeply. He spun slowly and shifted her body so he was able to reach down to his hip and retrieve a pistol before he lifted it straight out in front of him while silently taking a knee. The action had Shy lifting her head to stare in the direction his weapon was pointed.

For long minutes she didn't see or hear anything aside from the rustling of the wind through the pine trees over head. Then she picked up a low humming sound. As it got closer she realized it was an approaching vehicle. Before she ever saw it, York re-holstered his pistol and stood. When the jeep pulled out of the shadows with its lights off, Shy wondered how the driver was able to maneuver the vehicle through the dark woods, let alone find two bodies hiding in the brush.

The jeep pulled to a halt and York jerked the back door open before climbing in. He kept Shy on his lap. She recognized one of York's men as the driver. No words were spoken as they back-tracked for Tito then traversed the mountain side, finding a barely discernible road that led down to the highway and into a small town.

Chapter 3

Shy woke in a tiny motel room. It smelled of musty carpet and cigarette smoke that had long since seeped into the walls before going stale in refusal to disperse. The bed she slept on was small and a broken spring was jabbing her in the ribs. It was heaven! She'd given up hope of ever being freed from the Megalya facility. Now, her eyes flooded with tears at the simple pleasure of sleeping in a warm room on a mostly soft mattress. Her stomach grumbled and as she'd done so many nights before she simply ignored it.

"I'm glad you're awake."

The words pulled her attention to a chair she hadn't even noticed next to the window. York's massive frame barely fit in the weak looking piece of furniture. He had the curtain pulled back a fraction and was scanning the area.

Releasing the curtain he stood and stalked across the room to a table. Shy's eyes followed his movement and the instant she saw the bucket of chicken the scent of it hit her and had her stifling a moan of hunger.

York grabbed the entire bucket and fisted a handful of napkins before crossing to the bed and setting the chicken on Shy's lap. "Sorry, it's the best I can do right now."

With trembling fingers she reached up and grabbed a piece of the still warm, fried chicken and attacked it. Too hungry to care that she was acting like a starving refugee, she devoured two pieces before she finally looked up and bashfully held the bucket out toward York.

The behemoth smiled and shook his head before his look changed to one of pity. "Doc says you shouldn't stuff yourself. It'll make you sick after so many days without."

Shy pulled a greasy drumstick from between her lips long enough to ask, "Doc?"

York crossed back to the table and pulled a carton of milk from another bag. He handed her the milk and she quickly folded the top open before downing half the contents in one swallow.

"Easy," York admonished. "She said not to give you too much." He shoved an indecisive hand into his hair, "I promised I'd ration your food, but damn if you don't look ready to blow away." He went back to the chair by the window. Bending to place his elbows on his spread knees he faced her. "How often were you fed?"

"Usually every few days," she mumbled around a bite of food. "They started to feed me more the last few weeks. Not sure why," she lied before smirking, "Good behavior I suppose."

York watched her silently before he sat up, "Conn attempted to circle back with Leto, but they showed up on Canadian radar and had to hightail it across the border."

"Conn?" She remembered reading about him in the Walker files kept at Megalya.

"Commander Conn Drago. He led the mission. He's the best there is." York smiled then, "And when we get you back to StoneCrow, Commander Drago and his team will return to the Megalya facility and hunt down the rest of those fuckers. No one escapes Conn Drago."

Shy nodded. What were the odds there existed two Commander Conn Dragos? He'd been the one she'd researched while working for the Megalya. Her face twisted in curiosity. “What’s a Leto?”

York frowned. “Leto.”

He said it like she should understand and when she shook her head York stood and paced to the bed. “Leto Reigns. That’s the name of the other prisoner who was being held at Megalya.”

Realization dawned and Shy dropped her half eaten piece of chicken into the bucket before grabbing a wad of napkins and wiping her mouth then pulling the soft paper down each of her fingers. “H-how is he?”

She noticed that York seemed relieved that she knew of the other prisoner, but didn’t ask why.

York sighed loudly in relief and sat back down. For a moment, her question had him unsure if Shy even knew Leto, but once he’d stated that he was the other prisoner she’d clearly remembered him. It was typical for Walkers to be held captive and never relinquish their names to their captors.

"He's fine. A little undernourished like you and a great deal cranky, but no worse for the wear. With rest and food he should be fully healed in a few days."

"Fully healed?" Shy stopped cleaning her hands, "What did they do to him."

"Just tests. He refused and fought them on several occasions, but we heal quickly."

Shy dropped her eyes, "I never had any success with fighting them. Th-they only hurt me more." She stared at her hands.

"What kind of tests."

Her shoulders hunched as she tried to make herself smaller, "I-I don't know. Just tests. Lots and lots of tests. Whatever they were looking for or trying to do must not have worked. They weren't very happy with me."

"How did they capture you?"

Blinking hard Shy sat up straighter, "I don't want to talk about it." She wasn't about to admit to this relative stranger that she'd actually been a Megalya employee before they'd kidnapped her and experimented on her. She hadn't known what kind of monsters she'd been working for until it was too late and when she'd confronted them they'd been sure to make her pay. Her eyes scanned the room, "C-can I call my sister?"

He seemed disappointed to have to say no. "I'm sorry, but it'll have to wait until we're back to the States." Uncertainty warred on her tired features and York felt compelled to add, "You will be allowed to contact your family as soon as we get you back to StoneCrow. We need to ensure we're not being followed, which means all comms are down."

She eyed his hands, "How do you stay in contact with your men?"

He didn't want to have to explain the mystic—mist for short—that Skin Walkers used to communicate with each other telepathically. "Hand signals and gestures," he lied. He pointed to the window. "I have men stationed across the parking lot. They've got eyes on this room."

"Oh."

He relaxed, happy that she seemed appeased with the answer. Watching her, his expression shifted to one of concern as she yawned and blinked slowly. He got up and took the bucket of chicken from her lap. "Rest Shy. You need it. Don't worry, I'll protect you." As if to add emphasis, he pulled the pistol that was strapped to his thigh and returned to his seat to face the window. He peeled back the curtains and scanned the area. Shy reclined back on the bed and watched York stare out the window until sleep reclaimed her.

Chapter 4

"I don't know what in the hell you're talking about," Leto growled impatiently.

"Shy!" Conn growled, "You don't remember her? She's your angel!"

Leto slammed his hands down on the table and stood, slamming his chair back against the wall as his dark eyes locked on the large commando in front of him. "For the last time. I do *not* have an angel!" He wrapped a large hand around the halo at his own throat for emphasis.

A Skin Walker's halo was generated over time much like the antlers of a deer. Only the Walker could remove his halo and it was only taken off to gift to his angel, his mate. A Walker's angel experienced a transformation with the acceptance of the halo. Like their Walker mate, angels would become immune to illness and would be able to communicate with their Walker mate through the mist for short, their telepathic means of communication.

Conn leaned forward going nearly nose to nose with the Walker who was mere fractions of an inch taller.

"Conn!" Aries chastised grabbing her Walker husband's arm.

Conn eased back to put himself between Leto and his wife. He kept his eyes locked on Leto. "I'd have to be dead to forget about my Aries." He shook his head in disgust. "I don't know what they did to you in there, but my men don't lie to me. They have your angel, she carries your scent and like it or not *she* remembers *you.*"

The door opened and the CEO of StoneCrow entered smoothly wearing a dark suit. "Stand down Commander."

Conn growled but stepped back when Aries frowned and tugged on his arm.

"Welcome to StoneCrow Mr. Reigns. I'm Monroe StoneCrow." He gestured toward Leto's overturned chair, "Please have a seat."

Leto sneered from Conn to Monroe before relaxing his posture and unfurled his clenched fists. He bent to grip the overturned chair and his long satiny hair swirled around his arm in a glossy black tornado. He slammed the chair upright and dropped onto the chair crossing thickly muscled arms across an equally impressive chest.

"I've been informed you've refused to go to medical." Monroe grabbed a chair from where it sat against the wall and pulled it to the table to take a seat across from Leto with Conn and Aries still lingering at his back.

"I've just spent God knows how long being pricked and prodded by lab rats. The first person who comes at me with a needle fucking dies!"

Monroe shrugged, "Fair enough. Before you're taken to your quarters, I'd like to discuss your angel."

Leto growled and his dark eyes narrowed on the CEO as a rumble emitted from his chest.

"He doesn't remember her," Conn supplied accusingly.

Monroe frowned and turned to look at Conn. "Could York be wrong?"

"No," Conn didn't hesitate to answer. "He was with me when I found Leto. He knows Leto's scent. The woman has been marked by him," he thrust his chin in Leto's direction. "I might question it if it was York's word alone but Marko and Bodi confirm it as well."

"Lok?" Monroe asked.

"No," Conn responded, "he was with me but three's enough Monroe. She's his!"

Monroe turned to stare at Leto and watched as the man's jaw clenched. "Conn, take him to his quarters. Let's get our brother fed, hydrated, and rested. It's the best we can do if he refuses medical." He turned to stare at Commander Drago, "Have Chef Jenny Arkinson deliver his meal personally. Leto's been malnourished long enough, I want his needs met."

Conn's expression didn't falter at the CEO's subterfuge. Jenny Arkinson was a Walker and wasn't the estates chef but their resident chief surgeon. It was clear to both Monroe and Conn that something was wrong with Leto. There had to be for the Walker to have forgotten about his angel. Neither Monroe nor Conn scented a lie when Leto claimed to not know Shy so it was apparent that the Walker legitimately believed he didn't know his own mate.

Monroe stood and walked to the door where he was met by Conn. "Where are they?" Monroe asked in a hushed tone.

"The BlackBird went down just outside of Lethbridge. They're holed up right now. York's getting Shy fed and rested. She's so frail that he's afraid to move her right now."

Monroe nodded and rubbed at his smooth chin, "The Canadian military was prevented from pursuing you across the border but they did contact local authorities. It nearly turned into an international incident. It was smart thinking to fly below the radar once you hit the border. The Canadians appeared to be deceptive."

Conn rubbed the back of his neck, "I'm glad it worked. We skimmed more than a few pines making it back." His expression darkened, "I doubt I'd do it again."

"You won't have to. I want you to take a convoy to escort York and his team back, but they'll be driving not flying. Too many eyes on the sky right now.

Get Leto situated then get your ass up to Canada and get our Walkers and Leto's mate back here. I want it done ASAP."

Conn nodded.

"And I want it done quietly. No mistakes Commander."

Monroe pulled the door open and had just taken a step when he heard Leto's growl, "I'm going with you to Canada."

Leto had heard of Monroe StoneCrow and his estate that was a refuge for Walkers. It was the reason he'd come to the North West and it was the reason he'd been captured.

Monroe's eyes narrowed on Leto before he looked at Conn. Conn shrugged and said, "I'd want to go for my angel. He's welcome to come."

"Fine," Monroe bit out turning to Leto. "But not in this condition. Eat, shower, and rest. Commander Drago will retrieve you when it's time."

"I'm fine," Leto challenged.

"I won't have your health putting my men in jeopardy. You're welcome to accompany the team but only once you're rested and nourished. We're Walkers Leto, which as you already know means we're being hunted. You need to be able to back up my men and protect your own ass if shit hits the fan." Monroe turned and addressed Conn. "Get him settled. I'll contact Chef Arkinson myself. She'll be at his suite waiting." Monroe didn't look back as he stated loudly exiting the small interrogation room, "Welcome home Leto."

***

Shy woke to find York cramming gear into a dark rucksack. He smiled at her when she sat up.

"How you feeling?"

"Fine," she shoved scarlet hair from her eyes, "What's happening?"

"We're rolling out." York glanced at his watch. "Commander Drago's headed our way. They're going to meet us on the state side of the port."

It was too much information coming in too quickly. Shy rubbed her eyes and yawned. Her belly ached and she rubbed at it and frowned. "How long was I asleep?"

"Fourteen hours. You hungry?" He stopped working to stare at her in obvious concern.

Fourteen hours? Holy shit! "No," she rubbed her belly again and York's eyes followed the movement. He stood and rounded to the bed to tower over her.

"You okay?"

"I'm feeling a little nauseated." She hid a flinch at the telling confession.

His frown deepened, "I apologize. I shouldn't have allowed you to eat so much."

"It's okay," Shy mumbled relieved he thought it was from overeating. She sat up and was easing off the bed when all color drained from her face and she raced to the bathroom. The door slammed and York could only stare at it and listen as Shy got sick.

Shy lifted a shaky hand to flush the toilette as she got up off her knees and crossed to the sink before blasting on the water, washing her hands, and then cupping water to her lips to rinse her mouth. Gargling she repeated the action several times and then grabbed a hand clothe to wash her face. A knock at the door had her frowning at her wane image in the mirror. "I'm fine." She spoke loudly before she dropped to sit on the edge of the tub, uncertain if she was finished being ill.

"Shy?"

When she didn't answer the door clicked open and York watched her closely. "You okay?"

How could she be this tired when she just woke from fourteen straight hours of sleep? She lifted her head and met York's gaze. She knew she looked like hell, but it couldn't be helped.

"I'm just queasy is all," she lied as she forced herself to her feet. She'd been sick every morning for the past week and half; only difference was that today she actually had something in her belly to throw up.

"I'm sorry," he apologized as he entered with a blanket and wrapped it around her. "But we gotta move." He wrapped the blanket around her then scooped her up and carried her from the hotel.

Chapter 5

Leto frowned as they approached the small hotel nestled in the forest of Northern Montana. Instead of staying at StoneCrow and recuperating from his recent captivity, he opted to travel with Commander Conn Drago and his team of mercenaries as they trekked north to retrieve the woman who was also a captive at the Megalya facility and who apparently carried his scent. A growl escaped his parted lips. Every time he thought of the woman and what he'd been told of her, he growled in rage. She reeked of Megalya. How else could she carry his scent? He hadn't touched her and certainly hadn't claimed her.

After resting and being fed—well fed—at StoneCrow, Leto was feeling a hundred times better. He knew the unknown drugs that the scientists had injected into his system were slowly being burned off. In the meantime, Dr. Jenny Arkinson had been quite upset over his refusal to allow her to draw blood samples in hopes of pinpointing what it was exactly that the scientist had been testing on him. It hadn't taken him long to realize that the food delivery person was actually StoneCrow's Chief of Surgery, and after a dozen refusals, Leto finally jerked the syringe from her hand, jabbed it into his own arm and filled the attached vial with his blood before shoving it at her and growling, "You won't get more, so make it enough!"

She hadn't been pleased, but took what he'd offered with a promise to test his blood and have results by the time he'd returned with his angel. He'd fisted the halo that hung around his neck and challenged, "Does it look like I've claimed my one?"

He didn't know what the Megalya had done to infuse the other captive with his scent, but he doubted she was a captive at all. It made more sense to him that the Megalya would plant one of their own in the cells and pretend she were a captive in hopes that she'd be allowed to infiltrate StoneCrow when the Walkers came for Leto. They would know the Walkers would come. They always protected and defended their own.

"Easy," Conn urged addressing Leto and dragging him from his thoughts. "We'll be there soon. Once you see her I'm sure it'll all come back to you."

Leto frowned at the Walker commanding the mission. There was nothing to remember because he didn't know the woman. He'd shared his thoughts with Monroe StoneCrow about the woman being a Megalya spy, but the CEO had quickly shot down the theory stating that communications from a man named York confirmed that she was in too rough of shape to be one of Megalya's own. Monroe claimed she was 'lucky to be alive', which was enough to convince the CEO that she wasn't Megalya. Leto wasn't convinced and when he got to the hotel he had every intention of killing the Megalya spy who was so easily fooling his fellow Walkers.

***

After stopping at a café to pick up a large go-order and force-feeding Shy some toast, scrambled eggs, and a carton of milk, York and his team drove Shy across the border and to a quaint hotel nestled in the mountainside. Surrounded by thick forestland, the hotel would have been easy to miss had one not been looking.

Once again York's team checked them in before he'd carried Shy to a much nicer room then the one they'd stayed at in Canada. He told her to shower and handed her a sack that contained new clothing one of his team had purchased for her. She'd been rescued wearing nothing but the flimsy hospital gown the Megalya had provided. York promised to return soon with more food and left after showing her to the bathroom.

Shower? The thought brought tears to her eyes. At Megalya she'd been brought a bucket, soap, and a wash cloth only once a week. She hadn't stood under the hot spray of a shower since the morning she'd left her apartment for work and hadn't returned.

Before York departed he promised her that Marko was posted outside her door and Bodi was patrolling the perimeter outside. He'd sworn she'd be safe until he returned.

Once York left the room, Shy started a pot of coffee with the equipment and supplies provided in the room. She knew the caffeine would help revive her some, but still opted for decaff. The aroma had her belly convulsing painfully at the promise of the favored beverage she hadn't enjoyed in five months. She rubbed a hand over her flat tummy.

She savored a cup of coffee before creaming and sugaring a second cup and carrying it with her to the bathroom. Locking the door she turned on the shower and stripped while the room slowly began to cloud with heavenly steam. Rummaging through the toiletries provided by hotel she found a razor, tooth brush, tooth paste, shampoo, conditioner, soap, lotion, fluffy towels and an enormous fuzzy bathrobe.

Showering felt so good that after she'd washed and conditioned her hair, brushed her teeth, then shaved her body, she'd opted to wash and condition her hair a second time to delay having to get out. Finally, after long minutes she turned off the shower, dried, lathered herself with lotion, and then covered her naked body with the oversized robe with intentions of enjoying another cup of coffee while she waited for York to return.

She found a brush and for the first time in five months, brushed out her long red mane as hope blossomed within her. The

Walkers were taking her home and soon she'd talk to her sister and be back with her family.

The smile vanished from her face as the brush slid from her fingers and clattered to the floor. *Walkers!*

Shy had to grip the counter to keep from falling over as she remembered York's men diving from the helicopter. Contrary to what York had claimed, there was no way his men were wearing chutes unless the military had invented a chute that was so damn small that it was practically non-existent.

Shy blinked rapidly as she stared unseeing at her own reflection. Working for the Megalya, she'd studied the Skin Walker's incessantly, all while never truly believing that they could exist. The idea had been so outlandish and supported by no real evidence so Shy had immediately discarded the likelihood of their existence. She'd written off Conn Drago's rumored relation to Skin Walkers by his fierce reputation. After reading his military record, anyone could easily assume there was something supernatural about the highly decorated and now retired Marine. But what of everyone else?

Is Leto a Walker? Is that why he'd been held against his will and experimented on? If so that means that…she blanched. *York and his men are Walkers too.* Her hands trembled, *Holy shit, can they really exist?*

She tried to remember if she'd read anything about them being dangerous. Dr. Chambers had been certain that Walkers hated humans, so why were they tolerating her? She swallowed hard when she remembered York's words, 'My Commander has your mate."

Oh God! They think I'm dating Leto. They think I'm on their side through association. If they found out that she had originally worked at the Megalya facility things could be bad, but if they found out she had no involvement at all with Leto… She didn't even want to think of the ramifications.

Finding the bag of clothing she'd dropped in a chair outside the bathroom, she retrieved it and quickly dressed in the underclothes, tight jeans, t-shirt, and tennis shoes that York had purchased for her.

She had no idea that outside the hotel, Commander Conn Drago had just arrived with a very anxious and equally enraged Leto Reigns.

Chapter 6

Shy spun as she heard a key slide into the mechanism on the door and it beeped its admittance before the door to her room opened. She'd planned to be gone when York returned but she hadn't dressed quickly enough. Her heart skidded to a halt when York didn't enter, but a large, extremely attractive man with waist length, straight, black hair, and dark eyes that sparked with undisguised fury.

He growled before his expression faltered a brief second and he dropped to a knee. Light must have glinted off something around his neck and it temporarily blinded Shy even as she heard an odd high-pitched whine.

A vicious growl escaped the man's parted lips as his head snapped up, his eyes pinning her in place, one large hand fisting the shirt at his midsection. "What did you just do to me?" The words were growled from between clenched teeth, and if Shy thought he'd been angry when he'd entered, he was enraged now.

"I-I..."

The man's breathing hiked as he forced himself to his feet. He tried to hide a wince, but Shy saw it. He slowly approached and Shy felt sheer terror seize her. She recognized him…he was the Megalya captive she'd attempted to rescue. *Leto!*

Her eyes darted from Leto to the closed door. "S-sorry. I thought this was m-my room." She hoped to feign ignorance to escape. Dropping her head, she moved to step around him when he lunged to cut off her escape.

"What. Did you. Just *do* to me?" He growled a second time.

"N-nothing," she stammered while backing up several steps. "I didn't…"

"Lies!"

Shy considered screaming for Marko, but knew the Walker would have been aware of Conn and Leto's arrival. She'd find no help there.

"I'm…I'm sorry about the mistake," she apologized again, unsure what else to do. "They said this was my room." Unable to stand his hate-filled glare any longer, she dropped her eyes, "I'll leave."

"There's been no mistake," he growled seeming to compose himself some. The hand that had been clutching his stomach dropped to curl in a tight fist at his side. "They put you in my room intentionally."

Shy felt betrayed and knew she shouldn't. They all assumed she and Leto were an item. It would make sense to send him straight to her. She swallowed hard wishing York would return. "I-I don't know what you mean."

"You carry my scent Shy and as long as you do they'll all assume you belong to me."

Shy began to tremble visibly. *He knows who I am.* "I'm sorry. If you'll excuse me I'll…"

"You're not leaving. Not until I get what I want."

She took a step back until her legs hit the edge of the bed. She kept her eyes down, focused on the floor. She remembered hearing that Walkers carried many of the same instincts and characteristics as their animal brethren. She was being as submissive and non-assuming as she knew how to be. "W-what do you want?"

Leto was on her in a second. One moment she was cowering in front of him and the next she was pinned to the bed, her upper arms crushed under his rough grasp. His face was inches from hers and he sniffed at her loudly for long minutes before he sneered through gritted teeth, "I want the fucking truth. I know what you are and what you've done, and you're going to tell me why the Megalya are experimenting on Walkers or I swear to you Shy you will regret your silence. But first," his grip tightened on her arms, evoking a whine from her. "You'll tell me why you're infused with my scent and how you managed to injure me the second I walked in that door!"

Shy struggled under his grip even as his hips pinned hers to the bed. "Leto! STOP! I didn't do anything!" She watched as his eyes dimmed and he inhaled sharply.

"I don't even need to shift to smell your fucking lies."

Shift? It's true! Oh God, it's true!

A knock sounded at the door and when it drew Leto's attention. Shy shoved his massive chest with both arms forcing him off balance as she rolled and slipped off the bed. She was racing for the door when an arm clamped around her waist and hauled her back. As she made to scream, Leto's other hand covered her mouth as she flailed and kicked, fighting for freedom.

The knock sounded at the door again, and Leto growled impatiently, "What?"

"Everything alright in there?" Marko questioned from the hall.

Leto snapped his response, "Mind your own fucking business."

Shy's heart sank when she heard the footsteps stalk away from the door. Then she was flying through the air as Leto threw her back to the bed. She bounced and the back of her head smacked against the headboard drawing forth tears. Shy's hand reached to rub the back of her head even as she kicked her legs and scrambled backward trying to avoid Leto as he closed the distance between them and reached for her. She held out both hands defensively as she pleaded, "Please Leto, let me explain!"

"Lies," he growled, "that's all the Megalya deal in…fucking lies!"

Shy screamed as he caught an ankle and jerked her to him. "PLEASE! DON'T!"

Leto ignored her screams as he wrapped one massive hand around her throat. She'd seen the Megalya torture Leto; she knew well the expression that lanced across his rugged features. It was pure maniacal rage and she also knew from past experience that there was no controlling him when he was in this state.

She screamed again, but this time it was cut off as his hand tightened on her throat and she elected to conserve her oxygen as she clawed at his massive shoulders.

Seconds later his attention was ripped from her as he was suddenly jerked backward and wrestled to the ground.

Shy sucked in a harsh breath even as her feet found the floor and she raced to the bathroom. She slammed the bolt in place behind her, locking herself in as she quickly turned and scanned the room. She could hear Marko and Bodi trying to reason with Leto as loud crashing and the sound of shattered glass came from the other room. It wasn't working. Something crashed against the bathroom door and snarls erupted from the other room as Shy eyed the sole window.

She grabbed the handle and shook it furiously, but the window didn't budge. She heard York roar, "WHAT HAVE YOU DONE?"

Then another object shattered just outside the room. Shy snatched the towel from the wall ring next to the sink, wrapped it around her elbow and slammed it with all her weight through the glass before scrambling up through the window that was still lined with jagged glass before she dropped down the other side and out of the hotel room.

She ignored the pain that seared the crease of her inner thigh as she struggled to her feet and raced blindly through the forest. She ran as hard as she could and even though the ground was covered in snow and she had no coat she was sweating within minutes. She jumped fallen trees and ducked low-lying branches before she raced through an outcropping of trees and came face to face with a woman.

The woman was dressed in head-to-toe winter fatigues and when Shy saw the pistol holstered at the woman's hip, she wondered if the woman was a hunter. The beautiful stranger had jet black hair with one thick white streak that formed at her right temple and disappeared with the rest as it was pulled back in a tight ponytail.

Chapter 7

Aries' smile from mere moments earlier when her halo winked with its ethereal light and whined to signify the commencement of a Walker's affliction upon meeting his mate, vanished as she eyed Shy's tear soaked face, torn shirt, and the blood that soaked the crotch of the other woman's pants. Her fine brows drew down as her jaw worked. She'd heard the woman screaming earlier, and it took all her will to keep from storming into Leto's motel room and confronting him. "Did he..." Her words died off, she couldn't say it.

She must be a Walker. Shy dropped her eyes, shivering uncontrollably. Warm tears still slid down her face as she wrapped her arms around herself, "H-he hurt me."

Aries swore under her breath and swiped a small hand over her face. "Fuck!" She stripped off her winter-camo jacket and shoved it into Shy's hands. "Put this on." Aries' eyes swung round to quickly scan the perimeter as Shy slid her arms into the jacket.

Turning back to the other woman Aries pushed Shy's trembling fingers away and zipped the jacket for her. "How did you get out?"

Shy sucked in a shaky breath trying to stop her tears, "I-I climbed out the bathroom window."

Aries eyed the area again before sighing resolutely. "Alright, come on."

"Wh-where are we going?"

Aries grabbed the other woman's arm. "I'm getting you out of here. Now move. If Leto's not already after you he will be soon."

As they made their way through the thick forest, both women jumped and spun at the rustling of the trees behind them.

Shy was shoved behind the Walker woman as Aries spun and pulled her pistol simultaneously. Her sights leveled on RedKnife KillsPrettyEnemy as he stood scowling at the pair of women from the brush.

Shy's heart accelerated. She didn't want this Walker woman hurt because of her. She offered tremulously from behind the slight woman shielding her. “I…I don’t want to cause any trouble. I don’t want anyone getting hurt over me.”

RedKnife was silent as he eyed Aries and the gun she was pointing at him before his dark eyes slid to Shy and took in her appearance. His eyes lingered on the blood that stained the crotch of her pants. Then he looked back at Aries and slowly, silently back-stepped. Before he was swallowed by the thick foliage, he tilted his head to the heavens. His eyes darkened until they were a demonic looking solid black. Aries watched the Walker for several tense moments before he dropped his all black eyes to look at her. It was then that the snow began to fall thicker, in heavy near blinding sheets.

Recognizing the rare gift from the only known Indigenous Walker, Aries spun back to Shy and grabbed her arm, “Move!”

Aries sprinted through the forest and Shy kept up as best she could until finally she collapsed against a tree causing the Walker woman leading her to stop.

“What’s wrong?”

Shy drug her eyes up to meet the other woman's, noting that Aries wasn't even breathing heavy. "I'm tired."

Aries rolled her eyes, "Christ! Be tired later, he's coming."

Shy tensed and turned quickly to look over her shoulder before shoving off the tree and following more sluggishly after Aries.

They ran for what felt like an hour, but Shy knew it was actually more like a few minutes. Then Aries held up a hand and Shy skidded to a halt in the snow. She watched as Aries focused her attention on nothing in particular. When Aries was silent for several tense moments Shy whispered, "What are we doing?"

"I'm getting rid of my husband and his team."

Shy scanned the area confused before she remembered references to some bullshit theory that Walkers could communicate with one another telepathically.

Shy stood quietly behind the other woman and waited.

Aries blinked rapidly several times as if coming out of a trance before she turned to Shy. "We're going to have to run hard and fast. They're moving out but it'll only be seconds before they scent you and turn back. Are you ready?"

Shy sucked in a long breath and nodded, her eyes glassing up. She was running on pure adrenaline and even that couldn't keep her limbs from shaking from her exertion. She hated this. She hated running, hiding, and now the Walker woman with her was pulled into this mess deceiving her own husband. She wanted to apologize to the woman and thank her, but there was no time.

Aries curled her fingers in the sleeve of Shy's jacket as both women shot off at a break neck pace. Shy couldn't run fast enough. She was propelled more than actually keeping up on her own. The Walker woman was so much stronger. Shy hoped the day never came when the two were enemies.

Breaking through a stand of trees, Shy saw an army green jeep parked in the clearing. As they reached the vehicle Aries pushed Shy one way as she split the other. "Get in!"

Shy's ass had just touched the seat when Aries turned the keys that were in the ignition and slammed the shift into gear as the jeep jerked to life and the tires spun in the snow before catching and propelling the vehicle forward.

Shy braced one hand on the dash and another on the door frame. The vehicle rocked back and forth as it quickly descended the mountain. She stared at Aries and noted that the woman's eyes kept shifting to the rearview mirror and back. "Are they close?"

Aries slid her eyes from the mirror to touch on Shy's before frowning at the road ahead. "No, but they're coming now. They know you're with me." Aries' features cracked into a wicked grin then, "My husband knows I've deceived him. He's not happy."

Shy's heart squeezed. *What have I done?* She knew she had to take advantage of this opportunity in case… "Thank you for helping me."

Aries didn't respond, simply kept her eyes forward as she maneuvered the jeep over the slushy road.

"I'm sorry your husband is angry with you."

Aries grinned tensely, "I didn't say he was angry."

"He's not?" Shy asked hopefully.

"No," Aries stated. "He's fucking furious."

Shy's shoulders drooped as she slouched back in the seat. "God, what have I done? I'm sorry. I'm so, so…sorry." She shook her head then peeked over at the other woman. "My name is Shy."

"I know." Aries bit out tersely without offering her own name.

"W-who are you?"

"Aries. Aries Drago."

Shy couldn't control the gasp that escaped her parted lips. "Conn is your husband?"

Aries flicked a curious glance at Shy. "You know Conn?"

Shy shook her head immediately. "No. I've just heard York speak of him." She still wasn't ready to admit her role with the Megalya and the extensive research she'd done on the Skin Walkers. Silence filled the jeep before Shy spoke quietly, "Nobody can escape him."

Aries snorted before challenging, "I did."

"Maybe…" Shy licked her lips before continuing, "Maybe you should get out here." Her eyes slid to Aries' jaw as it worked angrily.

"With me you have a chance. If you try to run on your own, they'll have you before the sun sets."

"I just don't want you to be hurt because of me."

Aries scowled at the younger woman before biting out defensively, "Conn would never hurt me. No Walker man would hurt a woman intentionally."

Shy turned her head to stare out the window as Aries' eyes flashed to the other woman before sliding down to the blood that stained her jeans. She sighed heavily, "I'm sorry Shy. I've never heard of a Walker hurting a woman intentionally. I suppose Leto has just proved that it *is* possible."

Shy kept her eyes focused out the window.

Aries shifted gears and maneuvered the jeep off the snowy mountain pass and onto the wet highway.

Shy looked over her shoulder. "Are they still coming?"

Aries didn't bother with sugar coating. "Yes, but they had to back track for a vehicle. It'll buy us some time."

"Where will we go?"

"StoneCrow."

"NO!" Shy yelled, drawing Aries' confusion. "If...if we go to StoneCrow Leto will find me." It's where York had informed he'd intended to take her and she had no intentions of meeting him or any of the other Walkers there.

Aries' brows drew together, "It's alright Shy. Monroe will protect you."

Shy was shaking her head vehemently. She didn't know who Monroe was but it didn't matter. "You think one man can save me from Leto?"

Aries' eyes shifted to the rearview mirror again, "Monroe is not just one man. He's an army of Walkers unto himself. What I meant was that he *and* the others will protect you. Leto has no right to you, no rights where you're concerned. You're not wearing his halo. Even if he is afflicted, he shouldn't have forced himself on you. I've heard a forced claiming can happen, a Walker will force his angel's submission, but as I understood it took several months of her refusal to accept him. I didn't know it could be triggered so quickly." Her eyes darted to the blood soaked jeans again. "There will be consequences."

Shy stared at Aries dumbfounded before dropping her eyes slowly to her jeans and staring at the blood that darkened the denim. "Oh my God! You think that Leto…" Shy threw herself back in her seat and covered her face with both hands in mortification.

"What?" Aries demanded. "You don't have to cover for him Shy, you'll be protected."

Shy kept her head tilted back against the seat as her hands slid free of her face. Her skin had paled and she was shaking her head as tears slipped down her cheeks. "The man in the forest that let us go," she turned to stare at Aries, "he thought it too?" She didn't need confirmation. She knew he'd misunderstood.

Aries' knuckles whitened as she gripped the steering wheel harder, "While it's unacceptable in normal society, in Skin Walker society it's a crime that's punishable by death."

Shy gripped her stomach, "My God Aries! Leto didn't rape me!"

Aries turned to frown at her, "But you said…"

"I didn't say anything! You assumed. Fuck! This is bad!"

Aries frown slid from her face, "But what about the blood?"

Shy looked down and spread her legs apart fingering the tear in her jeans. "I must have cut myself climbing out of the window."

Aries' frown returned with a vengeance as she accused, "I heard you screaming Shy. You reek of his scent and your own fear."

"He was angry. He was…" the last word was barely audible, "rough."

"Fuck Shy, I'm risking the wrath of not only Leto but the wrath of Conn…pun intended. Did Leto hurt you or not?"

Shy grabbed Aries' arm. "He hurt me, but it wasn't like that! He was just so…so furious. He choked me. He wants me dead! Please don't take me to StoneCrow Aries. You said he has no right to keep me. I-I haven't done anything wrong. I can't go there. Not like this, not now. He'll kill me. He already tried, and if he finds out about the ba..." Shy gasped then realizing her mistake as she dropped her hands and pulled back into her seat dropping her eyes to the floor.

"If he finds out about what Shy?" Aries tone was firm.

"Aries I can't."

"They're approximately half mile behind us." Aries slowed the vehicle as Shy's eyes snapped to hers in silent plea. "Leto's with them."

Shy turned in her seat, "Please Aries! Please!"

"Talk," Aries demanded. "Leto will kill you if he finds out about what?"

Shy looked down at the speedometer, the vehicle was slowing rapidly, "Please just go and I'll tell you."

"Answers first!"

"Jesus Aries! Please! I'll tell you just go!"

Aries pulled her foot completely off the gas pedal and the motor whined as it slowed.

"BABY!" Shy shrieked. "He'll kill me if he finds out about the baby. I'm pregnant."

Aries mouth opened as she turned to stare at Shy in shock before she clamped her mouth shut and slammed her foot back on the gas pedal, pressing it until it was flat to the floor.

Shy watched as Aries focused straight ahead, her pupils expanding until her eyes were nearly black as she slowly inhaled. "I scent no second life Shy."

Shy lifted a hand to gently place it on her belly. "Well it's there."

Aries' tone softened "How far along are you?"

"I don't know. Five, six weeks maybe."

Aries' eyes crinkled at the corners, "Why would Leto want to kill you simply because you're pregnant? If anything that would keep him away from you. We should tell him."

Shy smiled weakly, the action not reaching her eyes. "I believe it's his child."

Aries' brows hiked, "Again I reiterate we need to tell him Shy."

Shy shook her head and began sobbing, "You don't understand Aries."

"Well help me understand damn it!"

Shy turned to Aries then, "Leto thinks I worked with the Megalya. He thinks I'm one of them."

"So tell him the truth. Shy if he's trusted you enough to sleep with you then he'll listen."

Shy threw up her hands in defeat, "He hasn't!"

"Hasn't what?" Listened?" Aries was completely lost.

"He hasn't slept with me Aries." Shy's lower lip trembled with the revelation as tears streamed freely and sobs wracked her slender shoulders. "The Megalya did this to me. They used his semen to impregnate me. He doesn't know I'm carrying his child. No one does." She dropped her head to stare at her belly before caressing it, "I carry his scent because I carry his child. He's never touched me until he tried to kill me five minutes ago."

Chapter 8

Aries nearly missed the curve in the road and had to jerk the jeep back onto the black top as she tried to regain her composure. "Shy I can't help you if you don't tell me everything. So please, start from the beginning and tell me all of it."

Shy wiped her tears on the sleeve of Aries' coat as she sucked in a shaky breath. She had to trust someone with the truth and the kind Walker woman next to her was as good a hope as any. "I was assigned to intern with the Megalya as part of my exit courses for college. I'd never heard of them, didn't know what they were."

"You were Megalya?" Aries' incredulous tone was accusatory.

"I was an intern. I didn't know what they were doing. I had to earn my last credits so I signed up for an internship. God, if I'd only known." She fell back against the seat shaking her head. "I'd heard them speak of their research on Walkers, Skin Walkers. I assumed it was all fictitious or at best some idiotic plot the military was working on for super soldiers that they'd attempt to execute and surely fail at sometime in the distant future. I didn't know that your kind actually existed. If I'd known…I never would have taken the position. I'm not evil; I don't want to hurt anyone." Her eyes flashed to Aries, "I *didn't* hurt anyone. I would never do that!"

Aries' eyes flashed dangerously then. "When you said you'd heard of Conn, was it just from York speaking of him?" She thought she'd scented the lie earlier but it didn't make sense at the time for Shy to lie about how she knew of Conn.

Shy shoved a hand into her hair. "They have files Aries. On all of you." She shrugged one slim shoulder negligently, "Well I assume *most* of you. There were so many… I never saw anything on you though."

"What information did these files have?"

"Everything. Height, weight, sex, appearance. It listed friends. They were trying to piece together relationships. I-I think they were trying to create a lineage. We focused on descendency, but they don't have much information in that regard. They're not sure who's related and who's married. I think they're trying to track the source."

"Source?" Aries scoffed angrily. "The source, or sources, are long since gone. Why in the hell would they care?"

Shy drew in a long breath, "Replication."

The word had Aries turning to her in horror. "Please tell me you're fucking joking!"

Shy's head dropped closer to her chest. "They abducted Leto and experimented on him Aries. When I tried to put a stop to it, they locked me up. They said they erased my identity, my bank account, my school records. I don't even know if I exist anymore. They locked me up and experimented on me too. They used me to test the viability of insemination using Walker seed." She shook her head dejectedly, "It worked and it's all my fault."

Aries' eyes grew wide in incredulity. "That's why Leto doesn't understand why you carry his scent? He doesn't know that they experimented on you with his seed!"

Shy nodded, "He's never touched me until today." She raised a hand to swipe at the fogged up window at her side, "But it's more than them just experimenting on me with Leto's seed." Silence stretched between them until Aries narrowed her gaze on the smaller woman.

"I'm carrying his child, and he thinks I'm one of the Megalya." She turned to Aries, "Fuck I am! I helped them Aries, I thought it was all just some ornate military bullshit. Some wanna be sci-fi break-through. I didn't know what I was doing. I was just supposed to find a compatible female for the sample. When none of the subjects matched I…I swapped my own DNA into the equation hoping it would work and I'd earn an easy 'A'. I didn't know…I didn't…"

"Jesus Christ Shy! We have to tell him."

"No. He thinks I'm Megalya. He'll think it's a trick. He'll never understand. He'll never trust me. He already wants to kill me. I don't care what he does to me," her tone shifted to one of resolve, "but I won't let him hurt my baby."

"Shy, I don't know what to do here. We can't run forever. Conn can track me easily. We're bound."

"Then let me go. Pull over and get out and I'll take the jeep and keep running." Panic flared to life as Aries slowed the vehicle. "What are you doing?"

"It's no use Shy. Leto's found us."

Shy turned to stare out the back window. "He's not there, we still have time. Just go damn it!"

Aries shook her head and pointed upward, "He's above us. The only reason he hasn't tried to stop us is because Conn's afraid his attempt would cause me to crash and Conn would never allow any harm to come to me."

"No! No, no, no, what do we do?" Shy was frantic now.

Aries stared at the other woman as the car slowed further. "We can't out run him Shy. We're nearly out of gas. He'll just stay overhead until the car dies. It's best we sort this out now with Conn close."

Shy's eyes were wide with terror, "Aries? You won't let him hurt me will you?"

Aries shook her head, "He won't hurt you again."

The setting sun cast a blood red hue to the wintry Montana Sky. It was rare to see the sun in the winter months and its uncommon appearance cast a foreboding chill as the jeep crawled to a halt.

Chapter 9

"What should I do?" Shy asked in sheer panic.

Aries slammed the gear into park leaving the keys in the ignition as she barked, "Stay in the jeep and lock the doors." She pulled the pistol from the holster at her hip as she jumped out of the jeep and slammed the door behind her.

Shy watched as Aries had her pistol trained on some unforeseen object circling the sky overhead. Shy shuddered and crushed herself into the seat as Leto dropped to the asphalt. She watched as he shifted from a massive bald eagle. Impossibly long feathers receded to smooth muscular flesh to form a kneeling man. Shy's eyes bulged in disbelief.

When Leto stood his clothes regenerated, wrapping around his corded limbs and torso to form jeans, hiking boots, and a tight black t-shirt. Despite the weather, he generated no coat or jacket. It was what he'd been wearing the day Shy had first seen him strapped to the table at the Megalya facility.

When Leto looked up, his brown eyes smoldered with rage as his eyes locked on Shy. Aries stood between Leto and the jeep with her pistol aimed at the Walker's chest.

Leto completely ignored Aries and any threat she posed as he growled at Shy, "Get out of the car."

Shy felt her breath catch as terror shot through her. She pulled her eyes from Leto to reach hastily across the driver's seat quickly locking the door before reclaiming her seat and locking the door at her side as well.

Leto's smile didn't reach his eyes. "Do you honestly think that's going to stop me Shy?" He took a step closer.

Aries pulled the slide on her handgun, chambering a bullet. "Back off Leto!"

His eyes reluctantly slid from Shy to frown at Aries. "*This* doesn't concern you."

"You're not going to touch her." Aries took a step closer, which garnered all of Leto's attention.

"Fine. I'll deal with you first then her."

Neither Walker seemed to notice the blacked-out four-wheel drive truck that screeched to a halt behind the jeep Aries had commandeered

Shy watched in relief as four men quickly exited the vehicle. All wore the same winter-camo fatigues that Aries donned.

"Do *not* threaten my angel Leto!" Conn's pistol was trained on the larger Walker.

Leto turned to Conn and dipped his head dangerously, "Do you really want to interfere in this?"

Conn didn't have to motion to his team. Lok, James, and Shane silently circled Leto until he was centered between the group of mercenaries.

Leto turned to sneer at the other Walkers. He knew what they were doing.

Conn holstered his pistol and held his hands up in a gesture of surrender, "We're not trying to keep her from you Leto."

"*That* is exactly what you're doing!"

Conn inched closer to Aries, "We're concerned about you. You've only just been released. We all know how difficult the captivity must have been."

Leto tilted his head, watching Conn with slight confusion. "You think I'm sick?"

Conn slowly dropped his hands as he side-stepped to stand directly in front of his wife blocking her from Leto's view. "It explains why you'd hurt your angel. You're confused."

Leto's eyes darkened furiously as his eyes slid back to Shy where she cowered in the jeep. "*That* is *not* my angel."

Shy flinched at the statement and dropped her eyes as she slowly slid from the passenger side to the driver's seat.

Anger was evident in Conn's tone as he challenged, "Of course she's yours Leto. She carries your scent."

Leto thrust a finger in Shy's direction as he bit out, "Touch those keys and you'll fucking regret it!"

Conn chanced a glance over his shoulder before turning back to Leto. "It's post traumatic stress disorder Leto. It's common. It's curable."

Leto threw back his head and laughed viciously before sobering, "I'm not psychotic Conn. That bitch bears my scent because she's Megalya."

Conn shook his head in confusion as Leto continued, "They experimented on me, took my blood. She already carried my scent when I met her, before I ever touched her. I did not bind her to me," Leto's eyes rested on Shy as his lip curled in derision, "I do not claim her. She. Is. Not. Mine."

Conn and his men turned then to stare accusingly at Shy causing tears to well in her eyes before they slipped free.

At Conn's back Aries whispered, "It's not what he thinks."

Conn turned to stare at his angel before stating without looking at Leto, "Regardless of what she is or what she's done, Monroe wants her brought in. We won't allow you to hurt her."

Leto smiled in challenge scissoring his massive arms in front of his bulging chest then behind his back as he prepared for battle. "Whichever one of you thinks you can stop me…"

"Shane." Conn didn't blink as a loud pop sounded milliseconds before Leto spun and caught the tranquilizer that had been aimed at his back.

Tranq still in hand, Leto turned to smile victoriously at Conn when two more simultaneous pops sounded and Leto's triumph shifted to surprise then rage as he stared down at the two tranquilizers that were pinned in his chest. He ripped the two tranqs from his body and sunk to his knees as he scowled up at Conn. Seconds later his massive form was huddled unconscious in the center of the road.

Conn holstered his two pistols and barked, "Get him in the truck, then double back for York and his team. We'll meet you at StoneCrow." He turned and grabbed Aries' chin gently, "And you, beautiful, have got some serious explaining to do."

Aries' eyes slid to where Shy was trembling and crying in the jeep. Conn's eyes followed and he whispered, "She's injured?"

"Yes."

Conn ground his teeth together, "Christ, I can smell her fear from here. I can't believe he attacked his angel."

Arie's hazel eyes frowned up at her mate. "It's bad."

Smoothing his thumb over his angel's bottom lip, Conn frowned. "How bad?"

Pulling her eyes from her Walker, Aries frowned at the jeep and the terrified woman within. "*Bad*!"

Chapter 10

Before they arrived at StoneCrow, Aries had called CEO Monroe StoneCrow on her cell, much to her mate's obvious displeasure. Shy was relieved to have heard Aries requesting asylum and protection on her behalf. The phone call had been brief.

Conn drove the jeep, traversing the icy roads, as Aries disconnected the call and smiled weakly over her shoulder at Shy.

When the trio finally arrived at the Skin Walker community Shy was comforted to find two women awaiting their arrival at the entrance to the large manor that stood majestically shrouded in the Montana forest, its stone wall façade lending aid to its apparent attempt at blending into the mountainside.

When Conn parked the vehicle and exited, opening the back door of the jeep to assist Shy out of the vehicle, she dropped her head and slid to the opposite seat. Ignoring Conn and his offered hand, Shy climbed quickly out of the jeep to stand close to Aries.

Aries led her to where the two women were standing. "Shy, this is Dr. Jenny Arkinson and Lilly Mulholland. Our Walker mates along with two other Walkers comprise the Board."

Lilly's aqua blue eyes and dishwater blonde hair made her seem less severe than the raven-haired doctor standing beside her. Shy nodded to both women, noting their beauty and the power they seemed to exude. None of the three women before her appeared in the slightest to be intimidated by their surroundings or the fact that a superhuman race roamed freely among them. In fact it appeared to be the opposite. The women seemed content and happy to have been drawn to their Walker mates.

Shy shivered at the thought of being drawn to Leto. He was stunningly handsome, but his sheer disgust and mistrust of her overrode any intention or even mere thought of a relationship where the Walker was concerned.

The dark haired doctor nodded to Aries misinterpreting Shy's tremor. "She's cold, let's get her inside."

Conn spoke from the back of the pack as the women moved. He followed them up the stone front steps and into StoneCrow manor. "Where are Monroe and King?"

As the doors to the elevator slid open, Jenny stepped in and walked to the back wall before turning, her lips pursed in disapproval, "Escorting your savage to the infirmary."

Conn's brows shot up in amusement as he stopped outside the elevator doors. "Why is he *my* savage?"

Lilly chimed in then her tone reproachful, "You Walker men are all the same. Attempting to force submission when it would most likely be given willingly if you'd simply ask."

Conn threw up his hands before winking playfully at Aries. "I think I'll join the other *savages* in the infirmary. I know hostile territory when I see it."

Aries grinned apologetically at her husband as the doors to the elevator slid closed.

Shy hardly got a word in edge-wise as the women all began chatting at once to devise a plan to keep her at StoneCrow and safe from Leto. She had suggested leaving, but it was quickly decided that the Megalya, knowing they'd successfully impregnated her, would be hunting her in full force.

Once it was decided that she'd stay, she interjected her terms. "No one else can know about the baby…especially Leto."

Lilly's expression saddened, "Are you sure Shy? Maybe once he calms down…"

Aries snorted as the trio stepped out of the elevator and crossed a cream carpeted hallway to enter a large empty office closing the door behind them. "You didn't see him Lilly. He's beyond depraved. He's certain she's Megalya and that she's done something to him." Aries turned to stare at Jenny, "Monroe needs to explain the affliction to him. I'm certain Leto hasn't been told."

"Affliction?" Shy lifted a hand to her belly in horror, "What is Leto afflicted with?"

Aries smiled, "Nothing," she eyed the other women knowingly over Shy's head, "it's just a term we use to describe…uh…*erratic* behavior in male Walkers."

Jenny reined in her smile as she cleared her throat, "Okay, no one can know about the baby and we give you asylum." She shook her head, "They'll find out eventually Shy."

Shy's eyes turned pleadingly on the woman, "Can't we cross that bridge when we come to it?"

Jenny stared at the other women for a few brief seconds. "Fine, but it's not enough."

Shy tensed, "What do you mean?"

Jenny looked from Aries to Lilly. "Without telling him of the child, we need another reason, an exchange of sorts. Monroe won't just grant her asylum. She's not one of us. We need something in exchange for the risk."

Monroe's voice had Shy and the other women turning to the door. "You'll need much more than an exchange."

As Monroe, Conn, and King filed into the room Conn and King noted that their angels, who typically gravitated to their husbands anytime they shared a room, were now taking a stance by refusing to come to their Walkers. Instead, the three women circled more tightly around Shy. It spoke volumes.

Annoyed, Monroe circled the women taking his place in front of his desk to address the room while Conn and King stayed by the door. King's eyes flicked affectionately over Lilly.

"We can't give her asylum. She's not a Walker," Monroe announced.

"She's an ally Monroe and *we* will give her asylum, or *I* will give her asylum."

Monroe's eyes darkened dangerously as he eyed his personal assistant, Lilly. "You think you have the power to protect her here?"

Lilly's lips curved in challenge as her brows drew together, "Mr. StoneCrow, you assume I'd stay here?"

Pain, then fierce possession raged across King's features as he uncrossed his arms and paced forward, taking a step closer to Lilly. "You will *not* leave StoneCrow!" It wasn't a request and it wasn't a challenge, the statement was made as a fact.

Lilly's smile vanished as she took a meaningful step away from King. "I'll not stay where women aren't protected, especially human women."

"You *are* protected," King growled menacingly.

Lilly's eyes slid from his to touch on Shy's bowed head. "*All* women."

King's hands curled into tight fists at his side. *Damn Leto!* "And how do you suggest I explain to our Walkers why we are protecting an admitted Megalya?"

Shy gasped and shot an accusatory look at Aries.

"She is no Megalya," Aries argued before shrugging and sending an apologetic look at Shy. "They had to know the truth."

"And she is no Walker either," Monroe countered. "I have no authority to welcome her here."

Lilly turned and pointed at Shy's belly, "She carries a Walker child Monroe. She *must* be protected!"

Shy felt the room spin violently. Not even ten seconds earlier, they'd agreed to keep the child a secret, now three more people knew!

Monroe and the other two men turned to stare at Shy. Monroe pulled his eyes away to look back at Lilly. "Why would

Leto harm a female that carries his child?" His face darkened dangerously.

"He...," Lilly looked at Aries then Shy before dropping her eyes to the floor, "he doesn't know."

"How can he not know?" King challenged.

Jenny stepped forward shrugging a shoulder, "They were kept in separate cells King. It wouldn't be difficult to keep it from him. Especially considering that she can't be that far along."

"So tell him," King urged, his brows spearing down in disapproval. "It'll solve everything."

"No, actually it won't," Aries opened her mouth to speak, but stopped when Shy jerked away from Lilly.

"Stop!" Shy's cheeks were flaming, "This is none of your business." She turned to frown at Monroe, then King, then Conn. "This is none of any of your business. If me staying here means you can all pry into my personal life then I'd like to leave...now!"

The room was silent as all eyes turned to Monroe. He watched Shy for several tense moments before turning to Lilly, "And if the child has no skill? If it is not a Walker?"

Lilly shook her head then, disbelief tightening her features and constricting her throat. Not all children that were born to human women mated to Walkers carried the Skin Walker traits. "What of me and King? Are you saying that if our Mahkya possess no ability, is not a true Walker that she and I have no place here?"

King growled and took a challenging step forward daring Monroe to denounce his angel or his child.

Monroe raked a hand through his hair angrily, "Of course that's not what I'm saying." His blue eyes slid to Shy, "I'm sorry, but we simply don't know if you can be trusted."

"I…" Shy began tentatively relieved that the men had backed off wanting her to tell Leto about the baby. "I can provide you with information in exchange for asylum. Just…just until my baby is born. But I went Leto kept away from me and he can never know about the baby."

Monroe's jaw worked before he demanded, "What type of information?"

Shy looked at Aries, hope springing to life. "They have files on many Walkers. I've read them. Most of them. I can tell you what they know."

Monroe's expression darkened.

"And they're doing research. I can tell you what they're working on, what they're looking for. I-I spent a year and a half with them, worked by their side. I know intimate details, layout of the facility, hierarchy of the staff. Most importantly, I know the information they have on StoneCrow."

Monroe's brows drew together, "They know nothing of StoneCrow!"

Shy shook her head, "Not the location or the name, but they are aware that Walkers are congregating, forming an alliance. They know you've started a…a colony."

Monroe cursed under his breath. "I'm not sure even that's enough to placate the Walkers here."

"Then let someone vouch for her." Lilly challenged drawing his gaze back to her.

“Who?” Monroe demanded, “Who do you think wants that responsibility? If she is here under deception it will cost her life and the life of whoever would be foolish enough to vouch for her Lilly. No one will take that chance.”

Lilly’s chin lifted defiantly and Monroe knew he was fucked. “*I* will take that responsibility.”

“NO!” King’s eyes darkened dangerously as he strode angrily to his wife and pulled her to him, clamping one hand at her lower back while the other lifted her chin until her eyes met his. “I will never restrict you in anything but this. You may not vouch for her my queen or anyone ever. I will not allow it.”

Lilly opened her mouth to argue, but was cut off as Aries stepped forward shrugging her shoulders indifferently, “I’ll vouch for her.”

Wordlessly Conn stepped up behind his wife. One strong arm pulled her back into his chest and the other covered her mouth as she struggled under his grasp, muffled cusswords still distinguishable. Conn scowled at Monroe and slowly shook his head. Conn too would not risk the life of his mate for an outsider.

Jenny who'd stood silently glanced at Shy with sadness on her face. She knew her Bishop would never permit her to risk her life to vouch for another and a Walker angel needed her mate's permission to vouch for anyone.

"You see Lilly there is no one willing," Monroe grinned then displaying his perfect white teeth, "or *allowed* to vouch for her."

"I vouch for her."

Aries stopped struggling under Conn's grip and all eyes turned to the door and Leto as he stood with his arms outstretched braced on either side of the doorway.

Chapter 11

Shy withdrew deeper into the room until she was partially hidden from Leto's view, her hand instinctively going to her belly as she bowed her head to keep from seeing him.

"How long have you been listening?" Monroe challenged.

Leto's outstretched arms shook as he made great efforts to keep himself erect. "Long enough to hear that you're attempting to release *my* prisoner under the guise of bullshit policy." Leto's jaw was clamped tight as he sneered at the CEO.

Monroe stood and strode closer to the door, putting himself between Shy and Leto to block the angry Walker from scowling at her. "You don't think Walkers will want her blood once they find out she's worked with the Megalya?"

Leto's eyes snapped to Shy and his lip curled back in derision, "She *is* Megalya?"

Shy winced and turned her back on the room.

"No," Aries countered, "she was an intern before they turned on her."

"Bullshit!" Leto challenged. A vicious growl sounded in the room before Shy heard Leto growl viciously, "I want her blood!"

Shy too moaned a fearful, "No!"

Monroe crossed his arms over his broad chest. "So you'll vouch for her to keep her here, hoping she is Megalya and will be put to death?"

"You just informed me that she *is* Megalya!"

Monroe shook his head, "We know she was in intern, we don't know the extent of her role and neither do you."

"I vouch for her," Leto reasserted. "Her true colors will show."

"It'll be your hide as well as hers if you're right."

Leto's arms were shaking more visibly now, the effect of the drugs still too potent in his system. "If I can end the life of even one of them than it's worth the sacrifice of my own."

Monroe uncrossed his arms, "Fine. You vouch for her. She stays. Clearly I don't need to explain to you the repercussions if things…end badly." When Leto merely continued to scowl at the CEO, Monroe nodded to King, "Help him back to the infirmary."

King was halfway to Leto when Leto ground out, "I want her taken to a cell!"

Monroe smirked at the other Walker. "That's not how it works Leto. You've vouched for her, which means she's welcome as a guest here until she *proves* to be disloyal."

Leto shook his head trying to force down the haziness that was quickly overtaking him. "She's already proven it!"

"She's admitted working with the Megalya," Lilly interjected, earning her a sour look from Leto, "that doesn't necessarily deem her as treacherous. If anything she's been open and honest."

King, not liking the look Leto was giving his angel, stepped in front of the Walker to block his view. "Time to go."

Leto growled his disapproval, shaking off King's hand as he turned and paced slowly down the hall using the wall for support. "Put her in a cell Monroe," he shouted from the hall, or I promise you, she'll make you regret it."

When Leto was finally gone, Monroe closed the door and turned to find Shy being cradled in Lilly's arms. "It's alright Shy. His bark is worse than his bite."

Shy looked up with wide pain-filled eyes and whispered, "He wants my blood."

"Well, he won't get it," Monroe bit out tersely.

All eyes turned back to the door when it was shoved open. Terrified Leto had returned, Shy buried her face in Lilly's shoulder.

"Is she alright?"

Instantly recognizing York's voice, Shy looked up in relief. The Walker was staring at her intently.

"She's fine." Monroe frowned and looked from York to Shy then back. "Commander." He nodded toward Conn and Conn stalked to York's side, gripped his arm and jerked the Walker behind him as both exited the room.

"Where's he going?" Shy asked. She'd grown comfortable with the tall Walker and had hoped he'd stick around in case Leto returned.

"Uhhh," Lilly's confused gaze flicked from Shy to Monroe then to the closed door. "They've got work to do."

Shy could tell that her inquiry about York had Monroe, Aries, Lilly, and Jenny on edge.

***

"What in the hell do you think you're doing?" Conn challenged as he forced York into the elevator, followed him in, and jabbed a button.

"I was checking on her." York was angry. He and his team had been stuck dealing with Leto while Conn, Aries, and Shy had preceded them back to StoneCrow. The entire drive he couldn't stop wondering how badly Shy had been injured. After Marko, Bodi, and himself were finally able to pin Leto down, York had kicked in the bathroom door and had been slammed by the scent of Shy's blood. Enraged, he could barely keep himself from attacking Leto. Shy was small and weak. It made no sense that *any* man would attack her let alone her Walker mate.

"Something's not right," York bit out. "Why did he attack his angel?"

Conn rubbed a hand over the back of his neck. "He's confused. He doesn't claim her and she's not wearing his halo." He cringed inwardly when he saw hope spark to life in his best friend's eyes.

"She's not mated?"

"She's mated York." Conn put a hand on the other man's shoulder and squeezed once before dropping his arm. "Leto's just confused right now. We all know he was afflicted the second he saw her again." He lifted a hand to his halo and stared sadly up at his friend. "The halo doesn't lie. She's his."

"If he doesn't want her…" York began but Conn cut him off mid-sentence.

"She's pregnant York. It's Leto's child. It's done. She *is* his angel." Conn could only watch in sympathy as York let his head fall back to stare up at the ceiling. The large Walker's shoulders slumped in dejection. "You'll find her York. Give it time. Your angel is out there somewhere."

"I thought…I felt…" he didn't finish.

"I know," Conn offered. "I know."

Chapter 12

"So," Monroe began angrily, "which one of you wants to explain to me how she is pregnant from a Walker who clearly despises her?"

Shy's gaze snapped to Aries and she shook her head hoping Monroe wouldn't notice the slight movement.

"Well uhhhh," Aries' eyes darted from Shy to Lilly who still stood with her arms around the trembling woman.

"Look," Lilly began, "she's had a rough day, rough week," she held Shy at arm's length to rake her eyes over the shorter woman, "hell it looks like it's been a rough year, plus she needs her wound looked at. Can't you grill us some other time?"

Monroe eased himself into a dark leather chair before propping his elbows on his dark mahogany desk and leaning forward in challenge. "No. I have a Walker willing to lay down his life on the bet that she's Megalya. She's pregnant with his child, clearly against his knowledge, and I want to know how she got that way!"

"The Megalya are attempting to create Walkers," Shy blurted out in hopes the diversion would work.

Something flashed knowingly in Monroe's eyes before he asked, "They want to create Walkers to find where our weakness exists? Are they searching for a way that would make us easier to kill?"

Shy shook her head, "You misunderstand. Their goal is not to kill you."

"Of course it is," King barked, "it's all they've ever done. What else could they possibly seek?"

Shy turned to frown at the Chief of Security before whispering, "They're trying to replicate the genes that create your…uhh, unique biological traits."

"Wait," Aries held up her hands, "I thought you said you didn't know what they were doing."

"I said I didn't know it was real. I saw the files Aries, they had me work on," she held up the first two fingers of each hand and bent them down, "projects." She sighed, "They want to be you."

“How close are they?” Monroe demanded.

“Not close. Hell, I didn’t even think it was real. They’d cycle animals through for some testing and it was laughable. The other interns and I thought it was a joke. But when they brought in Leto…”

Monroe stood, forcing his chair back. “Did you participate in the experimentation on him?”

“Me?” Shy’s eyes shot up, “NO! I didn’t…I wanted no part of it. As a matter of fact when they brought him in I demanded they release him!”

“And…” Monroe prompted.

Shy’s voice grew soft, “And they wouldn’t.”

Some of the anger left Monroe as he reclaimed his seat. “You’re right Lilly; it *has* been a long day. Jenny, see to Shy’s wounds and then Aries can take our guest to her quarters.”

“Come on Shy,” Lilly hooked an arm around Shy’s waist and turned with her.

“And Shy…”

She looked over her shoulder at Monroe.

"If you are Megalya and you're here to hurt any of my Walkers…," he smiled and flashed elongated canines while his eyes transitioned to a lethal black, "you *will* regret it."

Shy could only nod as she was led from the room. She didn't pay much attention as Aries, Jenny, and Lilly crowded around her on the elevator. All were silent and Shy kept her eyes down as she collected her thoughts.

She knew for the sake of her baby that she couldn't go home. If the Megalya were hunting her she'd never stand a chance, especially in her condition. With no other recourse, she'd have to stay with the Skin Walkers until her baby was born. Afterward, she didn't know what she planned on doing, but for now if they could keep Leto away from her it'd be enough.

"I can't fucking wait until he's afflicted," Aries spat practically grinding her teeth.

Jenny smirked, "I pray to God I get to be there to see it happen!"

"Me too," Lilly chimed in.

Lifting her eyes, Shy studied the three women in turn, "Who?"

"Monroe!" Aries ground out. "Son of a bitch is so unsupportive of mated Walkers!" She crossed her arms over her chest and drummed the short nails of one hand on her bicep. "But one day, he'll see what it's like."

"I hope it happens soon," Lilly huffed before drawing her brows together in concern, "poor woman. Whoever she is, I feel sorry for her already."

Jenny smiled mischievously, "I shouldn't say this but…" she eyed the women before her grin broadened, "there's evidence that suggests Monroe's affliction will be worse than most because he's the apex male."

"Affliction," Shy asked remembering hearing them say that Leto had been afflicted.

"Oh," Jenny's expression blanked, "never mind that right now."

Shy wanted to ask more questions about this affliction, but the elevator door dinged open and the group of women swept out.

"Okay," Lilly pulled her arm from Shy's waist. "Aries you go secure her room. I'm gonna go and get her something to eat while Jenny takes her to the infirmary and tends to her leg."

Jenny nodded and Aries chimed sarcastically, "Got it boss!" Aries wasn't one for taking orders.

Lilly rolled her eyes before smiling at Shy then stalking quickly down the hall.

"You got this?" Aries asked and when Jenny nodded Aries turned to Shy, "Jenny'll bring you up when she's finished. Don't worry, I'll be upstairs waiting."

Shy watched as Lilly turned and walked down the long corridor while Aries got back in the elevator and winked as the doors slid closed.

"Just me and you, come on." Jenny walked in the opposite direction Lilly had gone and without any other recourse Shy followed.

She was led through two swinging doors that led down another long corridor. Unlike the rest of the estate house, this section of the building had tile floor with cream-colored tile walls.

It felt sterile and when Shy saw a nurse coming toward them dressed in light yellow scrubs she froze.

No longer hearing Shy's steps behind her, Jenny stopped and turned to find Shy simply standing with a terrified expression on her now pale face. "Shy? What is it?"

"Where are we?" Shy asked tremulously.

"The infirmary." Jenny answered all matter-of-fact.

Shy's eyes quickly scanned the hallway, "Leto was going to the infirmary."

"He refused. King took him to his suite instead." When Shy didn't move Jenny added, "I really need to look at your leg, it's still bleeding."

Shy backed up a step, "It's fine." She turned and took two steps before Jenny's next words halted her.

"It's okay Shy, no one will hurt you here. Plus we need to check on the baby."

Shy's feet halted again as she lowered her head and lifted a hand to her belly. She hadn't had any prenatal care at all. She wasn't even certain the scientists at Megalya even knew she was pregnant, but she knew. She'd missed her period and had been ill every morning. Other subtle changes were also taking place and as much as she didn't want to be poked and prodded ever again, she did want to check on the welfare of her child.

"Just you?" she asked without turning back to look at Jenny.

"Just me Shy. I promise."

Slowly, Shy turned and reluctantly followed Jenny down the corridor and into a small exam room. Once inside a nurse entered before Jenny ordered, "Stoney, please leave us."

The nurse didn't ask any questions, simply turned and exited the room.

With a technique that showed years of experience, Jenny donned a lab coat, put on two surgical gloves, then pulled out a packet of stainless steel instruments that she arranged on a small tray and propped on a table next to the hospital bed.

"Have a seat," Jenny motioned toward the bed and smiled.

When Shy took a step toward it Jenny stopped her.

"Would you mind removing your pants first? I need to look at that cut on your inner thigh first."

Shy peeled off her pants, wincing at the sting on her inner thigh. Just dropping her jeans on the floor she kept her socks on and tugged her shirt down to hide her panties and upper thighs as she walked to the bed and climbed up facing Jenny before giving up on her modesty and reclining back on the exam table.

"So," Jenny began, "what made you decide to pursue a scientific field of study?" She scooted her chair closer and gently pulled on Shy's leg until she was able to get a good look at the wound.

"Are you seriously asking me about school?"

"Sure," Jenny shrugged, "unless you'd rather talk about Leto." A corner of her mouth tweaked when she felt Shy tense at the mere mention of his name.

"I wanted to do something that mattered," Shy answered. "I once naively thought that I could do something important, find a break-through in Alzheimer's, put an end to M.S., cure cancer."

She snorted at her once youthful ambition and lifted an arm to lay it across her eyes. "What a fucking joke."

"It's not too late Shy. You can still do work that matters."

"After seeing what they've done…the Megalya…I've lost all interest in the field."

Jenny worked quickly without looking up from her work as she spoke. "Don't let them do that. They've taken enough from you Shy; don't let them take your passion as well."

"It's too late, it's already gone." She dropped her arm and eyed the ceiling. "Simply being in this room makes me want to be sick. The instruments, the colors, the scent." Her lip curled in derision, "I hate it all."

"You know there are still good guys in the world Shy and we here a StoneCrow are some of 'em."

She felt Jenny's hands still momentarily before they continued their work. "As a matter of fact I could really use someone with your expertise her at the infirmary."

Shy shook her head, "I'm sorry, it's just…"

"Too soon?" Jenny supplied. "I understand, but in time if you happen to change your mind the invitation is open."

Jenny sighed then and stood to stare at Shy with compassion. She reached down to squeeze Shy's arm. "You'll forget about Megalya one day." She smiled then, "In the meantime, your leg is cleaned and sutured."

Shy sat up partially, "What? You gave me stitches? I didn't feel a thing!"

"I still carry a passion for my field and take pride not just in doing my job but in doing it well." She walked to a closet and rolled out a waist high machine with lots of wires. "Being in this room might be awful on you but I bet I can put a smile on your face." She plugged the machine into the wall and it beeped to life. "How about we get a look at that baby?" For the first time since meeting her, Jenny watched Shy's eyes light with joy.

Shy smiled and bit her lip to stop the action. She didn't want to hope for anything at this point. She knew better. Instead, she simply nodded and rolled her shirt up to just under her breasts as she reclined back on the table.

"Okay," Jenny rubbed some sort of lube on her belly, "but fair warning. You're pretty early so we probably won't be able to tell the baby's sex right now, so don't get your hopes up."

Drawing in a calming breath Shy nodded a second time.

Chapter 13

Leto paced in his suite, his long black hair trailing behind him as he stalked from the window of his suite to the front door then back. He'd slept through the night and when he woke the drugs that had been used on him had finally burned out of his system but something was off. His heart was racing and he felt panicky, anxious. He knew it had something to do with Shy because he couldn't stop thinking about her. He'd lost his cool when Conn had taken him to retrieve her from the Canada/Montana border and part of him regretted it. She'd been terrified but he couldn't stop the anger that surged forth when he finally got close and scented himself on her. He'd never touched her yet she did carry his scent. Even now he wanted to go to her and that angered him because he was trying to hate her. She was Megalya after all…wasn't she?

His eyes flicked to the clock and he wondered if she'd be awake. It was almost eight. If he started now before the other residents of StoneCrow manor woke, he knew he'd be able to track her scent…his scent as it were. Problem is he didn't know what to say. He couldn't understand why her admission at having worked with the Megalya wasn't a death sentence. Honestly, it had him questioning Monroe's leadership. *Fucking fool!* Still, he wanted to talk to her. He had dozens of unanswered questions and no one seemed willing to allow him to get them.

Inhaling sharply he slowly expelled his breath. The black tank top he wore stretched tight over his muscled chest and before he could reconsider it, he laced on his black boots and left his room in search of Shy.

***

In Shy's darkened room, Leto stood silently in the corner and watched her sleep. She'd been easy to find, too easy. It was almost as if Monroe had no concern at all that Leto would find her and kill her. A foolish mistake on Monroe's part.

Yet, here he stood. For some odd reason he couldn't stop staring at her. She was…beautiful. Her long fiery red hair billowed on her pillow and framed her pale face. Her full lips were parted as she breathed gently in her sleep. One arm was bent, her fingers almost brushing her lips while the other hand rested across her belly, the fingers of that hand splayed wide as if in her sleep she was making a conscious effort to keep her hand there. Strange.

She moaned and the sound brought his attention back to her face. She turned her head and her brows speared down. "No," she whispered and it was quickly followed by, "Leto, no!"

The sound of his name on her lips had his gut clenching. He wanted to do something but couldn't decide if it was wake her from her nightmare or silence her once and for all. The thought of hurting her more than angered him, it sickened him. He kept trying to will himself into just walking over, wrapping his hands around the satiny column of her throat and squeezing until she stopped breathing, but it was physically impossible for him to take a step. As a matter of fact, the mere thought of harming her actually made his stomach turn. He didn't want to hurt her, he wanted to shelter her and protect her.

His eyes lingered on the column of her throat and his tongue peeked out to wet his lips as he envisioned running his nose up her throat and following the path with his lips. He knew she'd be soft and warm. His eyes dipped to where her legs were spread under the blanket and when he imagined poking his nose and lips around in that region his cock grew painfully engorged.

He was shocked at his body's response to her and he stood breathing heavily in the corner trying to control himself lest he wake her from her sleep. *How can I want her?* He didn't understand it. *She's the enemy!* Strange how one's mind can know a fact but one's heart could be in doubt. He hated the contradictory feeling and emotions and he couldn't help but wonder if it wasn't some Megalya trick. Perhaps when they'd somehow infused her with his scent it drew some subconscious physical reaction from him.

She moaned and whispered his name again and his balls drew tighter. He curled his hands into tight fists and his eyes darkened. *If she says my name one more time...* He didn't finish the thought because it ended with him fucking her instead of killing her and he refused to be the Walker fool who was called in by some Megalya siren who'd somehow used his own scent to lure him in.

He watched as she kicked the blankets off and his eyes locked on her exposed legs and slid upward to the satiny powder blue panties she wore with a thin matching camisole. Her hand returned to shove her camisole higher and splayed slender, elegant fingers against her flat belly. He took a step closer.

Partially shifting, he inhaled. If they'd used his blood it'd surely dilute at some point and fade right? It didn't make sense that he'd scent this strongly on her. For a second he considered the notion that she too could have simply been a Megalya victim but the thought had his face screwing tight in rage. *That* is exactly what she wanted him to think. That she wasn't what she is…Megalya.

She straightened one leg then rolled to her side facing away from him and curled into a ball. Her panties pulled tight then slid over her luscious ass to expose more of her skin. If he didn't know for a fact that she was sleeping he'd think she was doing it to taunt him. His teeth ached from gnashing them together, but not nearly as badly as his balls.

Fuck I want her! He drew in a slow steadying breath in an attempt to calm himself.

"Leto," Shy moaned.

And that was it. Leto's control snapped.

***

Shy was startled awake and when her eyes snapped open they locked on the darkest most intimidating eyes she'd ever seen. She tried to suck in a breath to scream but the hand clamped over her mouth had her panicking momentarily until she realized she could breathe through her nose.

"Do *not* scream," Leto growled as he leaned over her.

Shaking her head she tried to convey that she wouldn't scream. She didn't know if he understood or not because his hand remained clamped over her face. Leto stared into her eyes for long moments and when they flooded with tears he tore his eyes away to study her face, then her hair.

He was on the bed with her, lying beside her. Well, partially beside her and partially on top of her. One of his legs was over one of her own resting between her thighs. The hand that wasn't clamped over her mouth was reached across her breasts and holding her shoulder in a firm grip.

Shy's breathing was rapid but nothing compared to the pounding of her heart.

With both hands occupied, Leto leaned down and used his nose to brush the hair away from the side of her face before dropping his head to inhale near her throat. He brushed his nose up and down her throat very slowly before pulling back to frown at her.

"You smell like you're mine." He licked his lips but didn't look away from her. "Are you mine Shy?"

Her name sounded odd on his lips. She dropped her eyes to his mouth and tried to place why it sounded so strange. It sounded…safe. She knew she should be terrified but was having difficulty conjuring up the emotion when he was being so gentle. It was a side of him she'd never seen.

"Answer me," Leto growled drawing Shy's eyes back to his.

*How do I…*she didn't know how to respond. If she said no she was afraid he'd kill her. If she said yes, then what? Would he kill her for saying it?

Slowly, Leto peeled his hand from her mouth finger by finger. It didn't happen slowly enough because Shy still wasn't sure how she was supposed to answer.

When his hand was finally gone she licked her dry lips and watched as his eyes followed her tongue. She swallowed hard, "Leto," his name came out more breathy than she'd intended. "Please don't hurt me."

His eyes flicked back up to hers, "Answer my question Shy."

She shook her head and her lips parted, "I-I don't know what you want me to say."

His expression darkened, "Speak the truth." The hand that was on her shoulder loosened and slid across the top of her breasts. The slow movement was sensual and had Shy's cheeks flaming as she felt her nipples pebble. She knew in the thin camisole the reaction wouldn't go unnoticed if Leto happened to look down. As if reading her thoughts his eyes slid down and locked on the stiff peaks that were now standing at full attention hoping for consideration.

"You react to my touch like you are mine."

His hand slid down over the thin material of her shirt and when his palm slid over one erect, sensitive nipple, Shy had to bite back a keening moan that nearly slipped free of her lips.

Leto cupped one breast before he began massaging it. Involuntarily, Shy arched her back and then quickly turned her head away from him to hide the mortification at her own reaction.

The hand continued to massage before it stopped to roll her erect nipple between two strong fingers. The sensation sent warmth shooting straight to her sex and when Leto added slight pressure with a pinch Shy couldn't control the eager moan when she knew she'd just moistened in preparation for him to take her.

Leto inhaled and the hand on her breast stilled then was gone. He grabbed her jaw and pulled her face until his eyes locked with hers. "You *smell* like you're mine."

“I’m sorry,” Shy whispered hooding her eyes under her lashes. “I am…” *God how do I put it!* “Attracted to you.” She cringed knowing she sounded like an idiot.

She felt his chest expand against her side, “That doesn’t answer my question Shy. Are. You. Mine?”

Lifting her eyes she stared at him, her vibrant blue eyes didn’t waver with the sad admission. “No,” her words were whispered, “No Leto, I am not yours.”

Chapter 14

With the admission that she wasn't his, Shy half expected Leto to snap her neck then and there. Instead, he jerked himself from the bed, punched a hole in the wall, then stormed out of her room, slamming the door behind him.

Shy hesitated only a moment before she reached for the covers and yanked them up to hide her half-naked state. She was still trembling and whether it was from fear, desire, or a mixture of both she wasn't sure.

Finally getting her breathing under control her heart seized when the bedroom door was thrown open and Aries rushed in.

"You okay?" Concern marred her brow as her eyes flashed down Shy then back up. "I just saw Leto storming down the hall. Did he hurt you?"

Afraid she wouldn't get the word out, Shy shook her head.

Aries turned to frown at the hole in the wall before looking back to Shy. "Did he *try* to hurt you?"

Again Shy shook her head. She didn't want to have to explain how Leto had snuck in her room to threaten her and had ended up getting her all hot and bothered. Licking her parched lips Shy dropped her eyes to study the quilt that covered her. "I-I thought you said I would be safe."

Aries planted both hands on her lean hips. "My room is just next door. I didn't expect Leto to actually track you down. It's foolish with Conn and his team so close by."

That caught Shy's attention. "Is York close?"

"Look," Aries crossed to the bed and took a seat. "You need to stay away from York."

"Why?" Shy's eyes rounded, "Is he dangerous too?"

"No, he's just..." Aries laced her fingers and stared unseeing up at the ceiling as if searching for the perfect word. When nothing sprang to mind she tapped her finger tips together while forming a silent "O" with her lips and shook her head before frowning and exhaling a harsh breath. When her eyes found Shy's she seemed annoyed. "Look, you know how you heard us talking about the affliction?"

"Yes?"

"Well, Leto is afflicted."

Shy flattened a hand on her chest and recoiled, "With what?"

Aries smiled. "The affliction in Walkers means that the male is in...," she dropped her eyes and blushed before peeking up, "heat?"

"Uhhhh," Shy's brows hiked. She didn't want to laugh at Aries but was highly tempted.

"Oh don't look at me like I'm a fucking idiot! It's true. Walker men go into heat. Leto's in heat, which means it's a really good idea to keep other Walkers away from you right now."

"What would Leto being in heat have to do with me?" Her cheeks flamed, "Aside from the fact that I'm a woman?"

"Here's the problem. You carry his scent because unbeknownst to him you carry his child."

Shy shook her head and shrugged her shoulders her face all but screaming, "And?"

"Leto's in heat and he's looking for a garden to fertilize. You carry his scent, which makes him think that you are his. So doesn't it make sense that the bull elk would go to one of the cow's in his harem when he had…needs?" Aries gave herself mental thumbs-up for having explained the affliction so eloquently.

Shy was in the process of scratching the back of her neck when she paused mid finger bend. "Did you just call me a cow?"

"Christ!" Aries threw up her hands and stood. "Look Shy, stay away from York. Stay away from all men unless you want Leto killing them. Because that's what he'll do. He'll be forced to assert his dominance and show that no one is taking what is his and he'll fight any and all challengers to the death. You are his and he won't tolerate another male near you. There! I said it. Do you finally get it?"

Fear inched up Shy's spine. "No. I'm not his!" She sprang from the bed and pointed at the hole in the wall. "Does it look like he's interested in me Aries? He wants to kill me! He *tried* to kill me! And you people promised to keep me safe and then let him waltz right in here while I was asleep. Do you have any idea how terrifying it is to wake up to a hand clamped over your mouth?"

Aries shrugged one shoulder negligently and mumbled under her breath, "Actually I do."

"What?" Shy snapped.

"Uh, nothing. Look, I get that you're confused and scared and all those girly emotions, but there are only two things you need to understand. One, stay away from other men. You'll only get them hurt. Two, Leto's a little…testy right now."

"Testy?"

"How about crotchety? Does that work better for you?"

Shy could feel her face reddening in anger. "He isn't crotchety Aries. He's a fucking psycho!"

"Well," Aries continued nonchalantly, "he didn't kill you so that's a plus."

"A plus," Shy gasped. "He didn't kill me and it's a *plus*?"

Aries winced, "Okay, that sounded bad. You know," she backed toward the door, "maybe I'll have Jenny or Lilly explain things to you. I don't seem to be doing a very good job.

"Yeah," Shy shook her head before covering a hand over her mouth then dropping it. "Maybe someone who is more in-tune with all these *girly* emotions I'm experiencing."

Instead of feeling bad Aries actually smiled, "Sorry. I don't do damsel-in-distress mode very well. But Lilly is just your girl. I'll get her. Stay here." And with that Aries backed out the door leaving Shy angry, confused, scared, and alone.

***

Conn found Leto in the estate's gym. The dark haired Walker was pummeling a heavy bag with such concentration that he didn't seem to notice Conn's approach.

"Ugh, ugh," Conn cleared his throat then threw up his hands when Leto spun on him with a fierce growl. "Easy Leto. It's just me."

"Leave!" Leto turned back to the heavy bag and started pounding away.

Conn circled the bag and braced hands on either side before stepping in to hold it in place with his hip. "So, you tracked down Shy."

Leto stopped punching for a moment. His angry eyes flicked to Conn then back to the bag.

"When I first met Aries, I was sent to retrieve her from the South American jungle. One of our Walkers has been searching for his sister. He had reason to believe that Aries was her."

Leto kept punching, "And I care why?"

Unperturbed, Conn continued as if Leto hadn't even spoken. "The very first time I laid eyes on her she dropped me to my knees." When Leto kept punching, Conn jerked back and yanked the bag out of his reach, which sent the Walker over extending and falling to his knees as his head snapped back and fury registered on his expression.

"Literally Leto. When I first saw Aries I was physically affected."

Leto's sneer faltered a moment as he remembered the first time he saw Shy. Quickly, he masked his curiosity and sprang to his feet to remove his gloves. "Again, I care why?"

"It's part of Skin Walker mating ritual. It's called the affliction. Mother nature's way of kicking us in the balls to ensure we aren't dumb enough to pass on our one true angel."

When Leto dropped the worn gloves on the mat at his feet and turned to head to the showers Conn's angry words stopped him. "At least hear what I have to say Leto. It might come in handy." Leto didn't turn toward him but he didn't leave either. "I'll tell you how it was explained to me but first I'll tell you that I didn't believe it for a second. I fought it. I didn't want to be mated, to be tied to any one person, but in the end…she was my angel and I couldn't just walk away from that.

Dr. Arkinson believes that the affliction is like the rut that elk experience; however, it's triggered not by the shortening of days but by introduction to one's angel." He stopped and eyed Leto's back. "Do you hunt?"

Leto didn't answer.

"Of course you hunt. We're Walkers, it's what we do." Giving Leto a wide berth, Conn circled until he was in front of the Walker. "A rutting bull elk is urged by his desire to ensure that his seed is passed on. Bull elk will fight for a harem and then fight to keep it. This ensures that only the seed of the strongest and most virile species is passed on. It truly is survival of the fittest and we Walkers are no different.

Like the rutting bull elk, we too will forego eating, drinking, and sleeping, too pre-occupied with protecting our angel."

"And if she *is* protected?"

Conn smiled. Leto's question wasn't confirmation that he understood or even believed his explanation of the affliction, but it was close. "It's more than just protecting her. The need to claim is what keeps the affliction from subsiding."

"Claim?"

"Mate," there was a smile in Conn's voice. "You can try to fight it. I did." He drew in a deep breath and exhaled loudly, "And I failed. The only thing I succeeded in was allowing my body to weaken to a point where I was unable to protect my angel when she needed me most. She almost died and it was my fault. I was too stubborn and too proud and it…" he didn't like to remember how badly Aries had been injured when Remy had taken her from him. He gnashed his teeth but smirked as it inspired a thought. "Shy is beautiful."

Leto didn't move, but his body suddenly tensed.

"There are many un-mated Walkers here."

Leto spun and growled out, "And?"

Conn shrugged, "Just saying." Deciding he'd given Leto enough information to process, Conn turned and left the gym without another word.

Alone, Leto sneered at the empty doorway and denied that he was drawn to Shy or afflicted by her in anyway. *Yes, she is attractive and maybe under different circumstances…* He pushed the thought aside still angry with himself at his body's reaction to her earlier that morning. *She is my enemy!* He repeated the thought in his head, much as he'd done the entire time he'd been working out in the hopes that the thought would finally stick and he'd stop thinking about Shy Brookes in any other capacity especially the one that had him fighting an erection.

She had done something to him, he was willing to admit that much, but he wasn't for one second willing to believe that she was his angel. *She's Megalya.* Why he was the only one that could see it he didn't understand, but he'd get the proof. He'd watch her silently from the shadows until she slipped up and when she did, he'd be the one catch her.

Chapter 15

Shy smiled as she gave Mahkya Mulholland a gentle push sending the little girl sledding down the slight snow covered slope and evoking a delighted squeal from the child.

"She loves it here," Lilly was re-packing the picnic basket she'd carried to StoneCrow park as she watched Shy inch down the hill to help Mahkya drag the sled back to the top.

"I can see why." Shy's cheeks were pink from the frosty exhilaration, her breath left her lips on a frosty cloud. "Thanks for the hot chocolate and sandwiches by the way."

"I thought a light snack would be nice." Lilly turned to her daughter, "You ready to go baby?"

"Aww, mom." Mahkya's lower lip pouted out. "Me an Shy was just havin' fun!"

Lilly smiled, "I know baby but it's getting cold fast and you need to take your bath."

"What about Shy?" Mahkya sulked, "Can she come over an play for awhile?"

Hooking the closed picnic basket over her arm, Lilly trudged through the snow to her daughter and grabbed her mitten-clad hand. "Shy needs to go back to her suite and get some rest. You remember I told you about the special package she's carrying."

Mahkya's eyes lit with excitement. "I remember momma." She smiled at Shy, "I hope it's a girl so me an' her can play together."

Shy smiled as she knelt to hug the little girl. "I do too. That would be really great." Pulling back from the embrace she smiled warmly, "Have a good day sweetheart and thanks for letting me come sledding with you."

"When it gets summer, we can come here and swing."

Shy stood and smiled at Lilly, "That'd be fun."

"Okay, well we're heading home. You sure you don't want us to walk you to the manor?"

"I'm sure," Shy replied, "It's not very far. You two be careful getting back home." She waved at Lilly and Mahkya's retreating backs. "Watch for ice."

Shy watched the mother and daughter walk away hand-in-hand and both longing and fear stole through her. Being pregnant was hell on her emotions. She was anxious and excited to welcome the baby but she was also terrified at the prospect of becoming a mother. Not to mention the fact that she'd been at Stone Crow for five weeks now and while they'd successfully kept the news of the baby from Leto, it didn't mean that Shy stopped being terrified that he'd find out.

Turning, she opted to stroll around the park before heading back to the manor. It wasn't even dinner time yet but the sun was already setting. Montana winters produced cruelly short days. Shy reached up to lift the collar of her coat higher in hopes of blocking the biting wind. She tucked her hands back into the fur-lined pockets of her jacket and quickened her pace hoping to get in a least one lap around the park before the cold forced her to find shelter.

While walking, her thoughts drifted to Leto—as they often did. She hadn't seen him since she'd woken with him in her suite. Aries had Conn place men on patrol outside her room and after two weeks when Leto hadn't reappeared the Walker Sentries were called off.

Aries had informed Shy that Monroe forced Leto into one of the cabins on the estate to keep him away from Shy. At first she thought he'd retaliate at being forced out of the manor but Aries reassured her that the cabins were much nicer than the manor's suites.

Shy's feet stuttered to a halt and the fine hairs on the back of her neck stood on end. It happened often. Quickly scanning the grounds she didn't see anyone. She never saw anyone, but she knew she was being watched…she could feel it.

Quickening her pace, she decided to cut through a heavily wooded portion of the park to make it back to the manor more quickly. Inside the thick brush, Shy stopped and held her breath when she thought she heard a twig snap behind her. She spun quickly but found no one.

Get a grip! She glanced at the sky and inwardly chastised herself for opting to take the walk. It was much darker than she'd anticipated and she hoped that the rapidly darkening sky was the reason she was freaking out. She considered backtracking out of the woods and taking the long way back and then just as quickly discarded the idea. Shooting one last look behind her she faced forward and took two steps before she gasped and jumped back when Leto stepped into her path.

His dark eyes carried their familiar disdain as they slid up and down her frame. She also noted that he looked tired and thinner…worn out.

"What are you up to Shy?"

"N-nothing." Her voice came out sounding too thin as if she were trying to hide something. "I'm not…I was just with Lilly and Mahkya. I'm going home."

"Home?" He took a step closer. "Is this your home?"

"I meant my suite," she amended quickly and dropped her eyes. "Excuse me."

Leto moved but not in the direction Shy had hoped. Instead of stepping out of her path he stalked closer until he was nearly touching her.

Shy made to take a step back but Leto's hands snaked out and locked on her hips holding her in place.

"What are you running from?"

She lifted her clear blue eyes to his. "I'm not running Leto. I'm not doing anything. I don't…want any trouble. Please let me go."

"I've been watching you."

The admission startled her. "W-why?"

"I told you I'd catch you when you slipped up."

Fear inched up her spine. "Leto I haven't…"

"Don't!" He growled. "Don't say my name."

Shy crossed both arms over her belly and dropped her head. She didn't look up even after several long minutes passed with Leto still griping her firmly by the hips.

Finally, he moved but it was only to lean in and brush his nose over her ear. He inhaled slowly and the proximity had Shy's skin warming.

"It's been weeks. Why do you still carry my scent?"

"I…I don't know," she shook her head.

A low growl was the only warning she got before one arm clamped around her waist and jerked her hard into him while his free hand reached up and wrapped around her throat forcing her eyes to meet his. He didn't apply pressure. There was only his touch. "You should know by now that we can scent lies. Tell me the truth. Why do you carry my scent?" His arm tightened around her middle and she flattened her hands against his chest.

"Leto…" tears flooded her eyes and she was on the verge of telling him the truth. Perhaps if he knew she carried their child he wouldn't just kill her in the woods as she feared he was about to. Before she could even formulate the words to explain it to him he quickly released her and growled viciously before curling both hands into tight fists and turning away from her. It was apparent from his posture that he was struggling to control himself.

"Run!" The lone world was growled at her from between clenched teeth.

Shy hesitated. She knew animalistic instincts demanded that predators hunt their prey *especially* if the prey ran. "Leto?"

Leto turned on her then, his eyes dark with rage as he snarled, "Get away from me Shy! Run! Because if you stay I'm going to do something we'd both regret!"

Shy stumbled backward before turning and racing through the woods. When she cleared the tree line she kept going. Not even bothering to look back she raced all the way back to StoneCrow manor. She slammed through the double front doors drawing the attention of several teenagers that milled about the lobby. Undeterred she dashed up the stairs to the second floor and down the hall to her suite. She had her key-card in hand before she even reached the door.

Quickly sliding the key card over the magnetic lock she thrust her body against the door the second she heard it beep. A sob escaped her lips as she lifted a hand to her belly. *He still wants to kill me!*

In the woods Leto still stood staring at Shy's footprints in the snow. He'd wanted to claim her so badly that he'd had to physically restrain himself from grabbing Shy, ripping her clothes from her delicate body, and mounting her in the damn park!

He'd scented her fear and knew instantly that she'd misunderstood his threat. It was just as well. He was having difficulty himself understanding the strange attraction to her. It had only gotten worse over the last five weeks. He'd watched her daily…stalked her. Convinced she was Megalya at StoneCrow to harm Walkers, he was disappointed and a little relieved that she hadn't attempted anything that he could deem a threat. In fact, she'd acclimated to life at StoneCrow rather well. She'd become fast friends with Lilly and Aries and she spent most of her days helping the two women with chores or tasks that aided the Walker existence on the estate.

Leto dropped to his haunches to trace Shy's footprint with a finger. He'd noticed that she'd gained a little weight and aside from diminishing the hollowness of her eyes and cheeks, it also filled out her figure in a way that had him clawing his hand into the frozen earth wishing he could explore her new fullness.

A glint of firelight caught his eye and he eased over to pluck the single strand of crimson hair from where it lay vibrant against the pale snow. Shy's hair fascinated him. He'd never seen anything like it. She preferred to wear it down and he preferred it that way as well. The satiny locks had gotten brighter and glossier over the past few weeks as she'd gotten healthier and now whenever he saw her it seemed as if her hair was alive. The unruly tresses shimmered and tumbled around her shoulders seemingly of their own accord. He longed to touch her hair and to run his fingers through the vibrant mane to see if it was as soft as it looked.

Slowly, he wound the piece of hair around his finger and lifted it to his nose where he instantly picked up Shy's scent. He was attuned to her now and she was quickly becoming an obsession. Conn had been right. He hadn't eaten or slept in many days and he was becoming restless…dangerous. He didn't really want to hurt Shy but the more he saw her the more he wanted to simply take her. He fantasized about it, even plotting out various escape routes if he decided to simply gag her and drag her away from StoneCrow and keep her for himself.

Maybe she isn't Megalya.

The thought instantly angered him; he was dropping his guard. His proximity to her was fucking with his head and making him forget his purpose for tailing her. He wasn't going to allow her to harm another Walker and he'd be the one to kill her if the Megalya somehow found their location. She didn't fool him. Leto dropped his head forward and rested his chin on his chest, vowing to steel himself against her beauty and allure. *She won't break me!*

Chapter 16

"Jesus Leto, you've got to do something!" Dr. Jenny Arkinson was more than a little concerned with the state of the Walker's affliction.

"Conn said that he denied it."

"No," Jenny jammed a needle into the Walker's arm injecting a specialized vitamin nutrient supplement she'd created specifically for hard-headed Walker's who'd rather suffer than claim their angel.

"Conn didn't deny anything. He fought it until he was too weak and exhausted and then gave in. When he was finally able to rest another Walker kidnapped his angel and she was severely injured. Aries almost died and I'm not saying it was Conn's fault, but if he would have just claimed her…"

When she pulled the needle out of his arm, Leto frowned at her. "Give me another."

"Look, I need to admit you. No one has ever gone this long before, not even Bishop. There could be side-effects, permanent damage Leto. You need to be monitored."

"No," he growled, "just give me more liquid food."

"It's not *liquid food*! It's a nutrient and vitamin supplement that isn't intended for prolonged use. It hasn't been tested in that capacity."

Leto held his arm up, "Test it on me."

"Leto, look..." Jenny didn't get to finish as a knock sounded at the door and it was pushed open without invitation.

Monroe StoneCrow entered wearing his typical tailored suit and flanked by his Chief of Security, King Mulholland.

"Morning Jenny," even white teeth bit into an apple as the CEO spoke around the bite. "Leto."

"What can I do for you Mr. StoneCrow?" Jenny's tone was clipped with impatience.

"Nothing. I've come to check on our guest, to see how his affliction is commencing."

"It isn't," Jenny began shoving supplies back into their assigned drawers and cabinets, her long dark pony tail falling over her shoulder to dangle near her hands as they worked. "He won't claim Shy and it's been too long." She turned and faced the men,

“I honestly don’t know how he’s even functioning. Bishop never lasted this long and the supplements,” she motioned toward the drawer she’d just closed, “weren’t intended for this. I can only assume that his metabolism has slowed due to his lengthy incarceration at the Megalya facility. Apparently it’s quite easy to ignore your body’s needs when you’ve been forced to do so for several months.” She narrowed her eyes on Monroe as she planted both hands on her hips. “You need to *do* something.”

Monroe smiled and took another bite of his apple. “Me? And what is it good doctor that you think I can do?”

“You know damn well you can force this.”

Leto growled. No one would be forcing him into anything.

Another crisp bite of apple sounded through the room while Monroe chewed and studied Jenny before swallowing, tossing the remains of the apple in the garbage, and then dusting his hands together. “Seems I won’t have to.”

“What?” Jenny shook her head confused, her eyes flicking to King at Monroe’s shoulder then back to the CEO.

“I’ve actually come here to inform Leto that he no longer needs to be concerned with Ms. Brookes.”

Jenny paled. She knew Monroe and his machinations well and she was terrified to find out where this was going. “Why?” she failed miserably at keeping the tremble from her voice.

Monroe ignored Jenny and instead focused on Leto. “As you’re aware Leto, our community here consists mainly of Walker males with few females and a handful of fully human staff. Shy has been here long enough to have drawn the attention of several males.”

Leto was surprised by the involuntary growl that passed his lips.

“Lucky for you, another Walker seeks to claim her and I’ve consented.”

“What?”Jenny shrieked.

Undeterred, Monroe continued. “Once he…mounts her, your affliction will begin to subside. It should only take a dozen or so *couplings* to rid her of your scent completely.

Jenny was shaking her head, her mouth gaping open in shock. The information Monroe was providing wasn't accurate. Not even close. There was only one way to sate Walker affliction and that was with the claiming and binding of one's true angel. Shooting her eyes to Leto she wasn't surprised to find him enraged. His breathing had increased, his brows had speared down, and his hands were curled into tight fists. Growls were rumbling from his chest and it had Jenny terrified.

She'd seen a Walker male in this condition only once before. Having run blood tests on samples, she'd discovered that she was Bishop's mate. Not wanting to be bound, she had one of her nurses put Bishop on a strain of extremely risky pharmaceuticals she'd concocted in hopes of preventing the affliction. When it didn't work, she'd had her staff keep Bishop in the dark regarding the affliction and put him on the same regiment of the vitamin nutrient supplement she was currently using on Leto. It lasted almost a month and a half before Bishop finally lost it and attacked her.

She now wore the double-helix of mated Walkers but she still hadn't forgiven herself for what she'd done to her Bishop. He'd suffered because of her and she'd suffered as well. She had to put a stop to Monroe's game. Whether he knew it or not he was putting Shy in grave danger. She knew better than anyone else.

"Leto, that's not true…"

King cut in, "I informed York that you'd granted permission." He directed his gaze to Monroe, "He's on his way to Shy's suite to claim her now."

The words were barely out before Leto jumped from the med bed and disappeared out the door.

"WAIT!" Jenny raced for the door, but Monroe's grip on her arm prevented her from chasing Leto. "What in the hell do you think you're doing," she spat. "He's going to hurt her!"

Monroe smiled but it didn't reach his eyes, "Walker men don't hurt their angels."

Sparks of fury burned brightly in Jenny's eyes as she jerked her arm free, "And how in the hell would *you* know?"

A muscle ticked in Monroe's jaw before he spoke. "King, would you ever harm your Lilly."

"*Never!*"

Monroe turned then, "You see."

"You need to send help over there now Monroe."

He stopped just outside the door to look over his shoulder, "I couldn't allow his affliction to carry on any longer Doctor. It was detrimental to his health."

"And what of hers? I know how you feel about humans Monroe, we *all* know, but have you no pity for their baby?"

"That baby is what's going to keep him from harming her and…" Monroe turned and began walking away, "it's what's going to bring that Walker to his fucking knees."

In the hall, King followed the CEO silently until they exited the infirmary. "You sure about this?"

"Sure? No. But we've no other recourse aside from losing him. If Shy believes Leto would harm her, then she has her own means of self-preservation."

"The baby?"

"Exactly. I'm not sure if he'd injure Shy. As Jenny pointed out, I've never been afflicted, but I do know that there isn't a Walker on the face of this earth that would harm a child."

"You're certain of that?" King smirked.

Monroe stopped walking and turned to level clear blue eyes on his Sentry. "Certain enough to have just bet Shy's life on it."

Chapter 17

Shy hadn't ventured out of her suite since her encounter with Leto. She knew now that the odd tingling sensation she'd gotten when she had been out had been caused by the fact that he'd been watching her. The thought still terrified her. She'd gone over the countless times she'd been out alone and played out every scenario of how Leto could have gotten her.

Huffing, Shy stepped out of the shower, dried herself, then smeared vanilla scented lotion over her body before wrapping the towel around her, tucking it in a tight knot just above her breasts. She shook her head frowning down at herself. "I swear they're growing."

Her breast size had increased by at least a cup and her hips had gotten an accentuated curve, but her belly—while slightly pooched—wasn't as pronounced as she thought it'd be by this point. She slid a hand inside her towel and rubbed a hand gently over her belly. "So what do you want for breakfast baby?"

Suddenly the bathroom door was slammed open. It crashed back and the doorknob imbedded itself into the wall sending dry-wall raining down on the crimson carpet.

Shy screamed as she spun towards the door. One hand instinctively clamping over her belly while the other latched onto the knot of her towel to ensure it stayed in place.

Leto's face was contorted in pure fury as he scanned the bathroom. He stalked to the shower and Shy had to jump out of the way to keep from being run over.

"Where is he?" With one jerk the shower curtain was ripped from the rod, the now empty rings jangling loudly in the small room.

"W-who?" Shy backed herself into a corner.

Leto growled and flashed his teeth, his canines had elongated. "York!"

Shy was trembling, "H-he's not here." She shrieked again when Leto grabbed her and pulled her hard against him.

"I heard you talking to him!"

“I-I wasn’t.” She shook her head vigorously, “I was t-talking to m-myself.”

Sneering down at her, Leto leaned down until his nose touched hers. “Do you always call yourself baby?”

“Leto, please?”

He released her so quickly that she stumbled back and had to throw a hand behind her and slam it against the wall to keep herself from falling.

Leto stalked out of the room. “YORK! Come out!”

Shy eyed the empty door way then slashed her eyes to her clothes folded neatly on the sink. She didn’t know if she should dress or run. She jumped when she heard glass shatter and she raced for the bathroom door, snatching her panties and bra as she went.

In the hall she could hear Leto slamming open doors and growling as he went. Quickly, she dashed toward the front door but didn’t make it.

“SHY!”

Her yelled name had her freezing on the spot. Too afraid to turn and look at him, she stood immobile. She expected to hear loud angry footsteps thundering toward her, but there was only deafening silence before a strong hand curved around her throat from behind then smoothed up to her chin where it gripped tighter and forced her to turn. Tear filled blue eyes met livid black ones.

"Leto?" She'd seen Leto angry, but never like this. He seemed…possessed.

"Where. Is. He?"

Shy licked her dry lips and swallowed hard. She noted that Leto's eyes locked on her lips and never moved. "He's not here. He hasn't been here. I haven't seen him since the day I was brought here. I…" she blinked and Leto's eyes left her lips when a tear streaked down her face. "I haven't done anything Leto. Please let me go."

The hand that held her jaw released and instead he lifted both hands to gently cup her face.

"I can't let you go," he growled inching his face closer to hers. "I can *never* let you go," the admission was pained as if it were a truth he didn't want to admit but could no longer deny.

Confusion struck hard and Shy actually felt bad for him when she saw the agonized expression he bore as he inched still closer. She knew that he hated her...*wanted* to hate her. Was it possible that he was battling his need to blame her for what had been done to him?

She'd thought of him often since the first day she'd seen him at the Megalya facility. Often? What a joke, she'd thought of him daily and since she'd been at StoneCrow that frequency had increased to nearly hourly.

Shy blinked as his eyes transitioned from an angry black. Liquid smoke swirled in their depths and she caught just a hint of amber and chocolate as his anger slowly receded. He was magnificent. His large frame pressed into hers and made Shy feel small and feminine and in need of protection...*his* protection.

He studied her as if trying to understand a highly confusing riddle. Was it possible that he was just as afraid of her as she'd been of him? Shy knew he thought she was his enemy. Megalya he'd called her repeatedly. Maybe if she confessed... Maybe if she told him of her involvement with the Megalya and exactly what it entailed. She swallowed hard as her breath mingled with his. Maybe if she told him about the baby. *Their* baby!

"Leto, I...," Shy's words were silenced when Leto's mouth slanted over her own.

He invaded the confines of her mouth and Shy was shocked by the earthy taste of him. It was enticing.

For a moment she stood immobile until something in his kiss had her reacting, licking him back tentatively at first then with more bravado. His taste was strange, not just the flavor of him but the sensation. It made her tongue tingle and her lips seemed to plump as his imploring lips continued their sensual assault. Without thought Shy's eyes drifted closed and she lifted her hands to wrap around his neck as Leto easily gripped her hips and lifted her up his body until her legs were wrapped around his waist.

He was strong and virile and the hard length of his body, his firm muscles, and domineering temperament had Shy fighting to think clearly. She wanted Leto, she had from the moment she first laid eyes on him but she knew the feeling wasn't mutual. So why was he here, kissing her, seducing her?

She felt them moving and part of her was afraid to know where he was taking her. Was this all a ruse to get her off guard and harm her? No, it wouldn't be. If Leto wanted her dead he could have killed her any number of times over the past few weeks. No, this was something else.

Leto growled into her mouth and the action had Shy abandoning all logic. It didn't matter why Leto wanted her just that he did.

Shy felt her hands slide across something cold before Leto was pulling back. Afraid to open her eyes and see the anger and regret she knew would be there, she opted to keep her eyes closed as she let her head fall slowly forward. She didn't want to face the rejection she knew was sure to come.

"Shy?" Leto's tone was impossibly soft and more gentle than she ever believed him capable of.

She refused to look up but opened her eyes to rapidly blink back the tears of disappointment that formed there. When her vision finally cleared Shy gasped to find Leto on his knees in front of her.

He'd carried her to the dining table and was now on his knees before her. Her legs had been spread when he'd carried her and still clad in only the towel, Shy blushed and tried to close her legs and use the towel to cover her exposed sex that had Leto's full attention.

Instead of allowing her to cover herself, Leto leaned closer so that his broad shoulders kept her legs spread and then forced them wider apart. His hands reached up and clamped over hers to keep her from hiding herself from him.

Slowly he lifted his eyes to hers. The struggle Shy saw there was heartbreaking. He was fighting something and she could clearly see it, but what?

"Why do you carry my scent?" The words spoken on a whisper were imploring, begging to be answered.

Shy opened her mouth and drew in a shaky breath. It was now or never.

As if sensing she was on the verge of explaining, on the verge of giving him the answers he sought but wasn't sure he'd want to know, Leto quickly pulled his eyes from hers and focused on her sex before pressing forward and burying his face between her legs.

She knew she was wet. She'd been ever since his lips claimed hers and when she tried to pull back so Leto wouldn't discover how he affected her, his hands locked on her hips and his nose pressed into her.

Shy arched her back and had no hope of stifling the keening cry of desire that escaped her lips when Leto's tongue sluiced through her wet folds. He lifted a firm hand to her chest and eased her back until she was flat on the table with Leto still buried between her thighs. His hot tongue seared through her again and she tried to clamp her legs closed to keep from coming at the sheer ecstasy his tongue provoked. His shoulders prevented Shy's attempt.

Still clamping one hand at her chest to keep the towel from slipping, Shy reached down and pulled on Leto's hair with her free hand, hoping to put some distance between his exquisite lips and her overheated flesh. Instead he growled and the sensation of the rumble against her pussy had her calling out as her eyes fluttered closed.

"Leto, please?" Shy wasn't sure if she was pleading for him to stop or to give her more. Her body was on fire and she ached to have him inside her. As if reading her thoughts, Leto's lips latched over her clit and began to suckle as one strong finger slid into her. It was too much. The sensory overload had Shy literally screaming. Involuntarily she bent both legs and braced her feet on his shoulders. Her hips bucked, urging him to move his tongue faster and he complied. Shy slammed both hands against the table allowing the towel to fall free as she thrust her bare breasts into the air when her back arched and she bit her lip to keep from screaming again.

Leto was relentless. His finger began to pump inside her then was joined by a second. He stopped suckling and purred against her sensitive clit and that was all it took for Shy to release her lip and scream as ribbons of ecstasy tore through her. The orgasm had her channel clenching Leto's fingers, attempting to milk his seed from barren fingers.

Shy's rock hard nipples were still thrust in the air and Leto's fingers remained deep inside her when her front door was slammed open.

Leto jerked his fingers free and spun on the intruder, his shoulders hunched as a ferocious growl was forced out of him. He turned to block Shy from view but still she gasped and scrambled to draw the towel up to cover herself as mortification seared her cheeks.

"Did you hurt her?"

Shy peeked around Leto to catch a glimpse of what had to be another Skin Walker. The man was just as large as Leto but where Leto's hair was long and black; this man's was shoulder-length and such a light blonde that it was nearly white. Shy's blush increased when Dr. Jenny Arkinson shoved the man out of the way and barked, "Get out of the way love, I have to get in there."

Jenny took one step before her eyes locked on the scene. Her mouth fell open and she gaped at Shy and Leto before the Walker behind her reached up and grabbed her arm. "I'm pretty sure we're not needed."

Jenny slammed her mouth closed and blushed herself before dropping her eyes. "Shy we heard a scream. Are you o-okay?"

Leto growled again and took a step toward Jenny and the Walker at the door. "Get. Out!"

The Walker pulled Jenny back until she was behind him. "We had to make sure she was okay Leto. We thought…" The man had the audacity to smile, "Well, we didn't think she'd be screaming from pleasure."

"Oh shut up." Jenny slapped the man on the back. "Come on Bishop, let's leave them alone."

Shy could no longer see Jenny behind Bishop but she did hear the offered, "Sorry to have interrupted." Then just as quickly as it was opened, the door closed.

Unsure what to say or how to react to what had just happened between them, Shy opted to keep her mouth closed and allow Leto to take the lead. Guilt gnawed at her for not being more forceful when she'd attempted to make Leto stop. The will and desire to stop him had fled almost as soon as his touch had gentled.

Staring at his back she watched his shoulders rise and fall rapidly and whether the action was a result of what they'd just shared or the confrontation with Jenny and her apparent mate, Bishop, Shy wasn't sure.

"Leto?" She whispered the word so quietly that when he kept his back to her she wondered if he'd even heard her. Shy inched toward the edge of the table but stopped when Leto spun and stalked toward her. Eyes rounding at the anger on his face, she gripped the towel tighter to her and shrunk back.

He was in her face, close, but refused to touch her as he growled, "If you seek release you *will* come to me. Stay away from York unless you want me to kill him!"

Then he stalked out the door and was gone.

Seek release? "Oh my God!" A hand reached up to clamp over her face as another wave of humiliation washed over her.

***

In the hall, Leto strode to the rail that ran along the second floor before he shifted and dropped in puma form to the first floor. His nails clawed into the plush carpet as he rocketed himself toward the front door. He needed to leave, to run, to do something, *anything* to cure the ache in his balls.

The animals raged inside him, demanding submission…Shy's submission. He wanted her under him, he wanted her wrapped around his dick, and he wanted her screaming his name. He wanted her and he had to get away from her before he forced what he wanted from her in an act he knew she'd never forgive.

He tucked his head and slammed his shoulder into the front doors as he raced through then he dashed across the lawn, cut across the parking lot, and cleared the few hundred feet to the thick tree line where he disappeared.

As he ran he went over everything that had just happened. When he'd gone to her suite he'd had no intentions of doing anything with Shy. His sole purpose had been to murder York, but when he wasn't there and Shy was wearing... He stopped his thoughts abruptly. The memories caused his balls ache and his dick hardened unbearably. Licking his lips his paws slid to halt when he realized the taste of her was still there. The sweet taste of her syrup had him shifting again. This time the puma's short hair bushed out as the large gray wolf tossed his head back and howled for all his worth.

Chapter 18

Leto hated taking orders especially from Monroe StoneCrow. It hadn't taken him long to realize the CEO and his Chief of Security had set him up. Somehow they knew that the threat of another Walker claiming Shy would send him racing to her prepared to claim her himself. And he had been. If Jenny and Bishop hadn't shown up... Shame seared him for the hundredth time since his previous night's escapades. He'd given in to his baser animal need to taste Shy and if he hadn't been stopped he would have most likely claimed her and bound her.

It had to be part of the Megalya experiment that he was now certain Shy and the Megalya were running on him. When in her presence he couldn't deny her. Even knowing that she's an admitted Megalya, even detesting her very existence when he thought of her, but one second in a room with her and his eyes were riveted to her. Not that she'd ever know. She always kept her head down, too afraid or ashamed to meet his challenging gaze.

Stalking down the hall to Monroe's office, Leto again attempted to fortify his resolve. *I will not look at her. I will not trust her. I will not want her.*

He didn't bother knocking when Monroe's words floated to him through the mist, *"Enter."*

Inside, Leto frowned at the CEO as he sat behind his desk flanked by both Conn and King.

"What?" The single word came out harshly.

"And a good day to you," Monroe scoffed without looking up from his paperwork. "Have a seat." He motioned with his pen toward a black leather couch that sat facing its twin, separated by a glass-topped table.

"I'll stand," Leto responded shortly. "What's so important you felt compelled to interrupt my afternoon meal?"

Monroe looked up then, a slow knowing smile spreading across his features. "There was no meal Leto. There hasn't been in days." The CEO leaned back and laced his fingers behind his full head of blue black hair. "I'd hoped to remedy that yesterday but as I understand your claiming was interrupted." His smiled faltered, "For that I apologize. Dr. Arkinson should have known better than to interfere." Monroe dropped his hands and shrugged as he loosed a resigned sigh, "Nonetheless, she knows now."

"Cut the shit Monroe. What do you want?"

Steepling his fingers over his pile of paperwork, Monroe's expression while appearing solemn didn't fool Leto. He didn't miss the flash of a quirk at the CEO's lips.

"The truth is you won't last much longer in your state. I can't allow a Walker to meet his demise due to his own…obstinance."

Leto tensed. Was he going to be challenged?

All eyes flicked to the door when it was clicked open and Aries Drago stepped through with Shy on her heels.

Leto's heart hammered ferociously at the mere sight of her.

***

Monroe sat at his desk with Conn and King standing on either side of him. Having been summoned and escorted by Aries, Shy stopped just inside the door when she saw Leto leaning against the far wall.

It had only been a day since she'd allowed him to bring her to release and Shy's cheeks flamed instantly at the erotic memory. Quickly, Shy ducked her head to keep the others from noticing even as her sex creamed with renewed desire.

Leto's massive arms were crossed over his broad chest and his eyes pinned her as she entered. His disdain for her was back in full force and was evident in the ever-present scowl on his face. Her eyes touched briefly on his before her gaze swept down, long auburn lashes veiling her uncertainty even as her body heated.

Shy felt Aries' reassuring hand on her shoulder. Fortified, Shy swallowed down her trepidation and slowly entered the office concentrating on the carpet as she walked.

"Shy, please have a seat." Monroe motioned toward two black leather couches that sat facing each other, separated by a glass topped table in the center of the room.

Shy moved to stand behind one of the sofas. She could feel Leto's eyes on her and her hand instinctively went to her belly before her fingers curled into the smooth cotton of her shirt. "Wh-what's happening?"

Monroe cleared his throat, "As you know when you and Leto were extracted from Megalya, boxes of intel were also seized. There's one piece of intel that I feel is imperative for Leto to witness to gain true understanding of the situation."

Shy chanced a glance at Leto. His cold brown eyes were still narrowed on her. Quickly, she turned to Monroe, "What does that have to do with me?"

Monroe lifted a remote from his desk and pointed it at the large flat screen TV that hung on the far wall. "You'll see."

The large screen flashed to life and Shy watched as a full color image of the Megalya facility came into focus on the screen. She knew the room that appeared. She'd worked in it often.

Several computers lined one wall, while along the other shelves of glass tubing and vials hung in rows the length of the room. The length of the counter beneath the glass held several microscopes, a calorimeter, and heated water bath. Nestled into the wall on either side of the counter was an operant conditioning chamber and a fume cupboard.

The scientists that milled about in white lab coats had been Shy's colleagues. Shy gritted her teeth as a man stepped into view of the camera.

Dr. Chambers had been the lead scientist at Megalya, and had been the one who'd ordered Shy's identity erased after they imprisoned her to use as part of their experiments.

The camera panned to the far right and centered on a panel of darkened glass. A light in the opposite room flicked on and illuminated the room housed on the other side of the glass partition. The small room held a single exam table with restraints attached for legs, arms, waist, and head.

Only the sound of the beeping of machines and mumbles from the scientists in the Lab could be heard. The observation room was sound proofed, which caused Shy to jump when the door to the exam room was kicked open and several Megalya soldiers hauled a shackled and enraged Leto into the room and forced him to the table.

Leto struggled and tossed two of the security guards to the ground before three more soldiers rushed the room to assist. In all, six soldiers were needed to restrain Leto and pin him to the table as the scientists moved in and strapped him down, one injecting a needle forcefully into his massive bicep.

Shy cautiously slid her eyes to Leto and watched his hands ball into fists so tight that his knuckles shone white with the force of his restraint. When Aries' hand landed softly on her shoulder, Shy turned back to the video as the camera panned left. Shy watched as she appeared on the screen. Her hair was pulled back in a careless ponytail and both hands were tucked into her lab coat as she entered the lab.

"Good morning Dr. Chambers," she greeted the Scientist who walked slowly to the glass partition to watch as the soldiers finally had Leto strapped to the table and began to file out of the room.

"Oh God!" Shy gasped turning to Monroe. "Turn it off!"

Monroe eyed her sympathetically, but his hand didn't move for the remote. Beside him, Conn shifted uncomfortably while King dipped his head and strode silently from the room.

"What's wrong?" Leto demanded, rage coloring his tone. "Afraid to face what you are…what you've done?"

Shy looked over her shoulder at the screen and watched as the smile slid from her face once she approached the glass.

"Dr. Chambers…what is this?"

Dr. Chambers smiled in triumph, "We have our first specimen Intern Brookes." Dr. Chambers glanced at her, "Isn't this exciting?"

Shy paled visibly as she looked from Leto struggling on the exam table in the opposite room to Dr. Chambers and his clear self-satisfaction.

"Damn it Monroe, turn it off!" Shy had inched closer to Monroe's desk and lunged for the remote.

Leto was on her before Monroe had risen from his desk. Conn's hand went to his pistol as Monroe held up his hand halting Conn from pulling the weapon.

Leto's hands crushed Shy's wrists as he spun her to face the screen. "You'll watch what you did!"

Shy was crying now, her head turning to the side as she pleaded, "Leto please, turn it off!"

Leto locked one hand around her waist while the other clamped on her jaw forcing her eyes back to the screen. "Watch Shy! See what kind of monster you really are!"

On the screen Shy flattened her hands on the glass partition. "He doesn't look like a willing candidate Dr. Chambers", shock and anger infused her tone.

The scientist smiled wickedly, "Sometimes sacrifices must be made for the betterment of mankind."

"Betterment of...You can't do this!" Shy made to turn, but the scientist grabbed her arm roughly.

"Please Ms. Brookes don't start acting like some sniveling sympathizer."

Shy struggled furiously under Leto's grasp, "Let me go!" She tried to force her head sideways, her eyes off the screen, but Leto tightened his grip forcing her face to remain forward.

"Dr. Chambers, take your hands off of me, and let that man go!"

Leto's grip loosened slightly and his gaze locked on the TV.

The other scientists in the lab stopped their work to stare up at Shy and Dr. Chambers as they squared off.

Shy yelped as Dr. Chamber's grip on her arm tightened painfully. "Or what Intern Brookes? You'll report me to your teacher? There are things going on here that are bigger than you and your pathetic excuse for an education."

Shy tried to jerk from his grasp, but he wouldn't free her. "I-I'll call the authorities," she threatened weakly.

Dr. Chambers' expression turned evil then as his eyes focused on something over Shy's shoulder and he nodded once.

Shy felt acid roiling in her belly at the memory of what came next. Pure mortification and horror seared through her. "Stop the video! Turn it off!"

Leto continued to hold her, his eyes riveted on the screen as he watched the never before seen footage of what had occurred in the lab while he'd been strapped to the exam room table.

Shy's eyes slid to Aries as she begged, "Aries? Help me! Turn it off! Please! TURN IT OFF!"

Aries moved for Shy when Monroe barked, "Aries stop! Leto needs to know."

Tears formed in Aries' eyes as she turned to frown at Conn before flicking a heated glare at Monroe then storming from the office, the door slamming behind her. Conn bowed his head and followed his angel out leaving only Monroe, Leto, and Shy to watch the horror on the screen as it played out.

Shy didn't see the two security guards until they were on her. She screamed and kicked as she was hauled from the room. One guard grabbed her feet and the other caught her under her arms. "STOP! STOP! YOU CAN'T DO THIS! HE'S A HUMAN BEING FOR CHRIST'S SAKE!"

The camera followed and slid to a second glass partition on the far wall before zooming in and focusing. Like Leto's exam room, this one also housed one exam table in the center of the small room.

Shy sobbed and jerked her chin out of Leto's grasp to turn her head, and this time he let her, his once bruising grip now slack. She couldn't watch what she knew was coming.

Dr. Chambers followed the security guards into the room and barked unheard orders. Like the other exam room, this one too was sound proofed.

Seconds later the guards were ripping the clothes from Shy's body, not caring if they hurt her or not. She fought them and was rewarded with a backhand to the cheek that sent her slamming into the wall before sliding down it and fighting to stay conscious. The guards removed the rest of her clothing easily, leaving her clad in only her bra and panties as they hoisted her onto the exam table where they strapped her arms, neck, and torso.

Shy felt a rumble in Leto's chest seconds before he released her and she crumpled to the floor. Covering her face with both hands as sobs racked her fragile body she whispered, "Please turn it off. Oh God, make it stop!"

Monroe turned and paced to the window, noting the horror that was now etched on Leto's face. He knew what the Walker was watching; Monroe had already witnessed the atrocities committed on the DVD.

Three scientists swarmed the room and took readings of Shy's vitals and several vials of her blood. They were more than rough. They were cruel. When a needle hadn't found a vein, one of the technicians removed it and stabbed her arms ferociously over and over before calming and trying again.

Shy's mouth never stopped moving. It was evident from her features that she shifted between trying to talk some sense into the scientists and screaming in agony.

When the scientists were fully satisfied with their readings, Dr. Chambers entered the room and had the guards spread Shy's legs and had them strapped to the gynecological stirrups that were pulled from under the exam table. Shy screamed, fought, begged, and cried as the scientist used a scalpel to cut her underwear from her body before the group began their extensive and lengthy exam. Shy was studied and probed against her will for long minutes before Dr. Chambers used a long stainless steel device to inject her with something.

Without words, Leto didn't know what the syringe held. He wouldn't know that this attack on her was the first of many that would finally succeed in impregnating Shy with his child. He would however know, once and for all, that she had suffered for attempting to free him. He would know that Shy was no Megalya, that she had cause to hate them more than any Walker ever would.

The screen went black and Leto stood for several silent moments staring at the screen trying to digest what he'd just witnessed. His eyes slowly slid to the creature that was huddled at his feet sobbing uncontrollably.

"It continues on like that." Monroe's voice was barely a whisper as he still stood staring out the window. "As you are aware it took us a little over five months to successfully extract you. During that time…," his tone was full of regret, "the experiments on her continued."

Leto didn't move. He couldn't.

Monroe turned to him then, "You see Leto, she is not our enemy, and you did not suffer alone."

Shy sawed in a shaky breath and wiped her face with her palms as she struggled to her feet. She stood facing Leto and she lifted her chin defiantly with more confidence than she actually felt, noting that for the first time since he'd laid eyes on her, Leto's ever present disdain for her was finally absent. Instead, shock and disbelief darkened the brown eyes that found hers.

Without a word Shy turned from Leto and as she took her first step to leave a sharp pain shot through her abdomen and sent the room spinning. Shy felt Leto's steadying hands on her as she stumbled. She made to shrug him off when the pain stole her breath. She felt her body crumpling even as the darkness consumed her.

Chapter 19

Shy woke in the StoneCrow Infirmary. A heart monitor beeped steadily at her side. As her eyes slowly focused, memory returned and her hand flattened on her belly as she quickly scanned the room. She was alone. Her hand found the nurse-call button on the side of the bed and she pressed the mechanism repeatedly until the door to her room swung open. Jenny walked in with her hair pulled back in a tight black bun. She carried an I-pad as she entered the room and smiled warmly at Shy.

"Good morning Shy…"

"The baby?" Shy demanded without preamble as she struggled to sit up.

Jenny's hands at her shoulders prevented her from completing the task. "Take it easy. The baby's fine."

Shy reluctantly relaxed against the bed, "What happened?"

Jenny smiled as she used her index finger to tap on the I-pad. "Stress. You've been under a great deal of pressure. *Too much* pressure for a woman in your condition." Jenny dropped the I-pad to stare at Shy. "When the body's had too much, it's had too much." Jenny shrugged, "You need food and rest. In that order." She lifted a hand to examine the saline drip that was injected into Shy's arm before stating casually, "Now that you're awake I'll have Leto summoned back to StoneCrow. He's eager to take you home."

Shy's soft features contorted in confusion. "Leto?" Shy shook her head, "Jenny, I think you're confused."

Jenny clucked her tongue, "Nonsense. He's been hunting the Megalya non-stop since you've been admitted. Granted it's only been two days." Jenny added absentmindedly before her brows furrowed and her tone softened, "I know what they did to you Shy. I'm so sorry you had to endure what…"

"Oh God, he doesn't know about the baby does he?"

Jenny smiled then it faltered, "Well…of course he knows." Her tone was laced with uncertainty. "We had to tell him, the baby was at risk Shy. He's the father, he deserved to know."

Shy threw her head back as tears formed. *Fuck!* She yanked the IV from her arm, "I need to speak to Monroe."

“Wait!” Jenny was trying to stop Shy from ripping out her second IV and detaching the heart monitor. “Shy please, I don’t want to have to sedate you.”

Shy slid her legs from the bed and eased onto her feet ignoring the doctor’s protests. “Monroe. Now!” she snapped attempting to steady herself as her legs wobbled beneath her. She felt weak.

The door to the room opened and it was two nurses that Shy had never met. One held a syringe and strode quickly toward Shy.

Shy spun, taking up a sharp pair of tweezers from a nearby table and wrapped an arm around Dr. Arkinson’s throat jerking the Doctor’s body into her own as she held the tweezers to the Jenny’s jugular. “Back off! I want a car out front, running with the keys in it, and I want it now!”

The smaller nurse smiled wickedly and shook her head, “We’re Walkers Shy. You can’t escape.”

“Stoney,” Jenny cut in reproachfully, “do as Shy requests.”

Reluctantly, the nurse, Stoney, dropped the hand that held the syringe and pulled the other nurse with her as she backed out of the room.

"Shy," Jenny began, "this is insane. Leto won't let you leave."

Shy shoved the Doctor into the chair in the corner of the room, still holding the tweezers extended towards her as she quickly checked the two dressers in the room and retrieved her clothes. "Look, I don't know which Leto it is that you've met, but the Leto I know wants me dead." Shy pulled on her jeans and stripped out of the hospital gown before tugging her shirt quickly over her head, and cramming her bra and socks into the pockets of her jeans. "As a matter of fact, he has tried to do the job himself on more than one occasion." Shy slid her bare feet into the tennis shoes she found next to the dresser as she motioned with the tweezers for Jenny to get up and lead her out the door.

"Honestly Shy, Leto's changed. You need to give him a chance."

Shy balled her fist in the back of Jenny's lab coat as she followed the woman down the hall. Several infirmary staff slowly appeared in doorways to watch the spectacle. "Give him a chance?" Shy laughed harshly. "Like the chance he gave me?"

Several times during the walk down the long corridor that led out of the infirmary, Jenny waved off would-be rescue attempts.

Outside, the sky was dark and a light snow slowly fell and dusted the earth. Stoney had delivered as ordered. A black sedan was parked in front of the building. The motor was running and the driver's side door was left open.

Shy scanned the area. All was quiet. Too quiet. She propelled the Doctor in front of her as she inched around the vehicle.

"Shy listen, you need pre-natal care. You're still too weak and too exhausted. All this stress isn't good for the baby. Please, just stay and let me help you."

At the driver's side door Shy stopped. She felt betrayed that a mere two days earlier Jenny had been willing to risk her life to protect Shy and now she was basically just throwing her to the wolves…well one wolf…Leto. "What do I need to know about the baby?"

Jenny shook her head, "How do you mean?"

"To take care of it," Shy demanded impatiently. "How do I make sure it's healthy? What do I need to know?"

Jenny licked her lips, "You need bed rest. And you're underweight, that's not good for the baby. Honestly Shy, if you stay I can…"

"What else?"

Jenny's brow furrowed disapprovingly, "You need to start taking pre-natal vitamins immediately. Seriously Shy, twenty pounds wouldn't hurt, thirty'd be great."

"Fine," Shy bit out, "Is there anything else."

Jenny's lips thinned into a line of disapproval. "As a physician I strongly urge you to reconsider your course of action here."

Shy snorted, ignoring the comment. "I'm going to need some money."

Jenny didn't hesitate to reach into the pocket of the slacks she wore. "You're in luck. The girls and I had a poker game planned for shift break." Jenny held up the folded bills and Shy grabbed the money quickly.

"I'll send you a check when I get where I'm going." Shy released Jenny's coat and shoved her forward before sliding into the driver's seat. "Where am I?"

Reluctantly, Jenny supplied, "The Highwood Mountains, just East of Great Falls."

Shy nodded.

"One more thing," Jenny quickly grabbed the car door before Shy had a chance to close it.

"Fuck, what?" Shy's eyes scanned the area fearfully.

Jenny smiled then. The excitement and brightness of her smile was so genuine it had Shy pulling back from the woman. "It's a boy Shy. You're going to have a son!"

Shy stilled, shock keeping her from moving.

"You should know, I haven't informed Leto of the baby's sex." Jenny continued proudly, "He'll be the first male Walker born here at StoneCrow."

Shy gave Jenny a somber look, "No, he won't. My child will not be born here." Shy pulled the door closed and clicked the electronic button, locking all the doors before she raced from the estate.

Jenny watched the taillights as she crossed her arms over her chest and rubbed her arms in an attempt to fight the chill of the snowy night. "Stoney?"

The Walker nurse stepped from the shadows behind her, "Yes Chief?"

"Contact Leto, let him know his angel has checked herself out of the facility and is currently en route off the estate."

"Already done."

Chapter 20

Shy had no problem at the main gate. She suspected Dr. Arkinson had advised them to have the gate open as a safety measure for the sake of the child. It was a foolish mistake on the Doctor's part, for as much as Shy wanted to be free of StoneCrow, she wouldn't risk her son's life to do so.

She slowed her rate to maneuver the winding mountain road that led down and out to the highway. There had been a map of Shonkin at the Megalya facility along with dozens of other maps of small mountainous areas where the Megalya suspected the Walkers were taking refuge. By some miracle, Shy's heritage touted Blackfeet ancestry, which had led her to study only one map, the map of Shonkin, as it was the Blackfeet word for High Woods. She knew where she was and how to get to the nearest town.

Once on the highway, Shy stayed within the speed limit. There was no point in risking her life or her son's. If the Walkers wanted to follow, they'd do so effortlessly regardless of the pace she set.

A son. One hand slid to rub comfortingly over her belly as she sucked in her bottom lip. *Oh my God! I can't believe it! I'm going to have a son!* The dawning realization conjured up tears. *What will he look like? Will he be healthy? What will I name him?* So many questions and too few answers. *First things first. I need to get to town and I need some food.* Her stomach rumbled its concurrence.

I wonder if he'll grow to be as handsome as his father. Her lips curved into a rueful smile. From the moment she'd laid eyes on Leto she'd thought him handsome, and now that she'd seen him without his scowl, she found him even more attractive.

His too black hair seemed to mirror his constant too black mood. Yet, she knew that in the breadth of his arms, under the unrelenting watchfulness of his gaze, some lucky woman would one day be sheltered. Even his warm brown eyes that had scowled at her with such disdain, still showed promise of softening for the right person. Regret seared her chest with the knowledge that it would never be her.

Quietly, Shy followed the highway she remembered led to the nearest town. Once a set of headlights had shone in her rearview mirror for several miles, convincing her that she was being followed, but eventually the lights disappeared as the vehicle behind her turned off on some rural road.

Ahead, bright lights formed a faint glow in the distance indicating that she was nearing the town. The knowledge helped relieve some of her tension. Finally, after almost an hour she passed a lit sign that read, 'Welcome to Great Falls'.

Just inside the city Shy breathed a sigh of relief when she found a café with a large neon sign under the name indicating the restaurant was open 24 hours. It was 11:30pm when Shy pulled into the parking lot.

She circled the building and parked behind it in an effort to hide the vehicle from the view of the highway. She found the button that popped the trunk and exited the vehicle to search for a coat. The temperature had steadily decreased in the time she'd been on the road. Shy rubbed her arms frantically as she stared down at the empty trunk. Slamming the trunk closed, she peered into the backseat of the car. *Shit!* No coat there either, she had no choice but to do without.

Shy crammed her hands into the pockets of her jeans. One hand pulled out her bra and her socks while the other fished deeper coming up with the wad of cash she'd taken from Jenny. She quickly thumbed through it. *$46.00? Christ!* It wouldn't get her a place to sleep for the night, but it'd get her fed.

She entered the restaurant and headed straight for the restroom. Inside she locked herself in a stall and quickly put on her bra and socks before using the facility and washing her hands.

Staring in the mirror she sighed roughly at the sight that met her. She was sickly pale except the dark circles under her eyes. Her cheeks were sunken and for all her pinching, she couldn't manage to bring any color to her them. She gave up on her face and raked her slender fingers through her hair in effort to tame the long auburn locks. *What I'd give for a steaming bubble bath.* She managed to crisscross the strands into a loose side braid before she was satisfied enough to leave the restroom and find a table.

“Hi hon…just one?” The stout older brunette waitress asked as Shy approached the ‘please wait to be seated’ sign.

“Yes.” Shy followed the woman to a table near the windows that overlooked the highway.

“Um, sorry...”

The waitress turned to frown at Shy.

“I forgot my coat. Is there any way I can sit someplace a little warmer?”

The waitress slid her eyes down Shy’s petite frame before turning from the window seat and leading Shy to one closer to the counter. “Good Lord girl, you’ll catch your death of cold.”

“Thank you,” Shy murmured as she slid into the booth in the center of the restaurant. She hadn’t avoided the windows due to the cold weather, she simply didn’t want to be seen should any Walkers drive by searching the area.

The waitress slid a menu onto the table. “Can I bring you something to drink?”

"Coffee." Shy replied instinctively, taking up the menu. As the waitress turned Shy caught her, "Wait! Can you make that hot tea instead?"

The waitress didn't look at her, simply penned a large 'X' on her pad and wrote something beneath it, "Not a problem."

Eyeing the menu Shy discovered just how difficult it was being responsible for the life and health of another human being. Her mouth literally salivated at the thought of pancakes, eggs, and bacon, but she quickly flipped the page away from the breakfast section knowing her son deserved something more nutritious.

When the waitress returned with a mug of steaming black tea, Shy placed her order. "Sirloin steak, wild rice, steamed veggies, and a cup of hot chicken noodle soup to start."

The waitress waddled away while Shy tried to convince herself that steak wasn't too far off from a mound of syrupy pancakes. Her mouth disagreed, but her conscience was eased by her choice. Her lips quirked ruefully. She had enough people angry with her; she didn't need to be mad at herself too.

She wrapped both hands around her mug of tea absentmindedly to warm them as she thought about her future. She knew she needed to contact her sister as soon as she got the chance. First, she'd need to think of a lie. The truth, horrific as it had been, would only incite her sister to call out the National Guard.

Shy dropped her chin into her upraised hand as her elbow rested on the table. She didn't want to relive the atrocities that had happened to her and Leto at the Megalya facility, and she certainly didn't need any national attention drawn to a child that was the product of artificial insemination from a never heard of shape-shifting species. No, she'd tell her family that her son was the result of a raucous night of sorority-girl life. While her mother certainly wouldn't approve, it was definitely a thousand times better than explaining the truth.

Her soup finally arrived and Shy savored every aromatic spoonful until her dinner was served. The sirloin steak, while not large, was cooked to a medium rare perfection. It seeped savory juices as she cut into it. She took alternating bites of her steak and wild rice before she attacked the bright pile of steaming vegetables on her plate. By the time she was finished, not a single piece of broccoli, cauliflower, or carrot was left on her plate.

"Any dessert hon?"

Shy dabbed her mouth with her napkin, "No thank you. Say, would you happen to know the name of a cheap motel in town?"

The waitress eyed her over the tablet she wrote on, "The motel on 15th isn't bad. Cheap, but clean."

Shy winced as she pulled eleven dollars from her stash to pay for dinner plus two dollars for a tip. Then she held up the remainder of the cash, "Thirty-three dollars kind of cheap?"

The waitress stopped writing to eye Shy suspiciously, "You in some kind of trouble?"

Shy shook her head, "No! No, just…passing through and need a cheap place to stay is all."

"Well," the Waitress frowned bracing both arms on the table, "I don't know where you're traveling to, but I doubt thirty-three dollars is gonna get you there." The Waitress passed a cursory glance over the restaurant before leaning lower, "Look, if you're having….*man* trouble. There's a shelter down town. No questions asked." The waitress stood and jotted something on her pad before ripping a sheet from her tablet and handing it to Shy. "Here's the address, just let them know you need a place for the night. They've even got clothes they can give ya'."

Shy could feel her cheeks singeing a bright red as she dipped her head to inspect the scrap of paper. *Christ lady you have no idea the kind of 'man' trouble I'm having!* "Th-thanks."

The waitress took the empty plate and coffee cup and strode to the counter as Shy quickly rose and exited the restaurant.

Inside the car she shivered as she waited for the vehicle to warm up. *Damn Montana winter!* Her breath was coming out in cloudy puffs and the vehicle was taking too long to get warm. She left the keys in the ignition and exited the vehicle intending on going back inside the café to wait for her vehicle to heat up.

"Hey pretty lady, need some help?" A large man wearing a cowboy hat and a long black duster stepped from behind a semi-truck cutting off her path to the café.

"No thanks," Shy answered politely trying to pass him, "Just gonna wait inside for my car to heat up."

The man's hand snaked out and caught her arm causing Shy to cringe. Ever since she'd been assaulted at Megalya she hated being touched, especially by men.

"Don't touch me!" She barked instinctively trying to pull from the man's grasp.

The man's grasp tightened, "Hey darlin', no need for hostility. Just trying to help keep you warm is all."

"Take your hands off her!"

Shy didn't need to look over her shoulder. She knew the voice, and by the sound of it, Leto was pissed!

Chapter 21

The cowboy jerked Shy to his side and looked up at Leto. "Why? She yours?"

Shy was startled when she was jerked to face Leto. He was angry but for once it wasn't directed at her. It felt…nice. *God he's beautiful!*

Leto didn't respond, simply dropped his eyes to the hand that was still crushing Shy's arm.

The cowboy turned to Shy then, "Is that your man?"

"No," Shy responded pushing on the cowboy's chest in attempt to shove away from him before responding angrily, "but you're not either so let me go."

The cowboy smiled up at Leto, "See friend, she's not interested in you."

Leto didn't say a word. One minute Shy was trying to wrestle free of the cowboy's bruising grip and the next thing she knew the cowboy was on the ground out cold. Leto rose from where he was hunched over the man's unconscious form and slowly approached Shy.

She took a tentative step backward, then another as she slowly backed away from him.

Then the waitress burst out the doors of the restaurant, "Hey, what's going on out here?" She looked at the cowboy on the ground and saw Shy backing away from Leto. "Honey is that the abusive boyfriend?"

Shy felt humiliation wash over her as Leto's expression darkened and he titled his head to stare at her accusingly. "Th-that's not what I told her Leto."

Shy heard the waitress yell over her shoulder, "Jimmy call the cops!"

Shy held up her hands as she continued to back away from the large Walker, "I-I don't want any trouble. I'm just leaving."

"With something that belongs to me?" His tone was harsh, accusing, but the hatred that typically burned in his eyes when he looked at her was absent.

Shy dropped her hands to cover her belly and spoke softly. "Th-the baby's mine Leto."

Leto froze then, his eyes shifting and he inhaled slowly before dropping his eyes to where her hands attempted to shield his child, their child. "Mine!" The word, while barely audible, was laced with conviction and carried to Shy on the cold wind that stung at her cheeks and held the faint sound of sirens in the distance.

If only she could bide her time until the police arrived. The thought died nearly as soon as it was formulated. Leto would kill the men before allowing them to take him in. Shy's eyes dropped to the unconscious cowboy still sprawled out in the snow. She watched his lifeless form for several tense moments, and she sucked in a sharp breath when she failed to see his chest rise or fall indicating he still lived.

Her eyes shifted to Leto, imploring him. "You have to let us go Leto. The police are coming."

He advanced a step, his eyes still locked on her abdomen. "*Never!*"

"Jimmy, Ronnie get out here!"

Shy felt panic flare to life. *You stupid bitch!* Shy cursed the waitress silently even as guilt washed over her. She knew the waitress was only trying to help, but anyone that stood in front of Leto right now risked his life by doing so.

When two young men shot out of the restaurant Shy held up her hands and screamed, "STOP!" She was trembling even as she spoke, "It's…it's okay." She turned imploring eyes to the Waitress. "Please, all of you go back inside. This has nothing to do with you."

"Look honey," the waitress challenged propping one hand on her ample hip, "We won't let him hurt you."

Leto turned his head as if finally realizing he and Shy weren't alone. The sneer that formed his features indicated he didn't appreciate the woman's insinuation, but his words fortified the look, "She carries my child." He turned back to stare at Shy, "I don't hurt what's mine."

"Hey," the Waitress yelled, "She's a person too Mister and she has choices."

Shy shook her head, "Jesus! Just stop." She frowned at the waitress.

"She does have choices." Leto responded to Shy alone, drawing her eyes back to his. "Right now Shy you have two choices."

Shy gnawed her bottom lip nervously.

"Either get in the car or I'm going to kill them all and *take* you to the car." He didn't smile as he held her gaze.

Shy eyed him then turned to stare at the group that was speaking among themselves formulating some plan. Shy cringed when she thought of the outcome. No matter what they did or how many there were, it would all end the same. They'd be dead and Leto would have her. Or she could go with him now peacefully and spare the lives of the three morons that had foiled her escape with what they perceived as a kind gesture.

Shy's eyes shot to the road just behind her. She wasn't sure if the police and their fire power would stand a chance against an angry Walker, but with them still not in sight she was rapidly running out of options.

"Shy, you have five seconds to decide then I start hurting people."

"Honey?" The waitress called.

Shy watched Leto's jaw bunch in annoyance as he spoke, "I'm going to start with her."

Shy lifted terror filled eyes to Leto then let them slide to the trio still standing in front of the restaurant before being drawn back.

"Three seconds."

"Okay!" Shy wrapped her arms around her midsection and dropped her head as she whispered, "Fine Leto. I'll go with you, just let them be."

He turned sideways and Shy inched slowly past making her way to the car.

"Honey you don't have to do this!"

Shy didn't even look at the waitress as Leto opened the passenger side door ushering her inside before closing it just as quickly behind her. He crossed to the other side quickly and within minutes they were back on the highway headed straight back to StoneCrow.

The ride was long and silent. Shy kept her eyes glued to the window, her arms still wrapped over her belly.

Leto cast her a sidelong glance before reaching down and flipping the heater to high. "Where's your coat?" His tone held that familiar condescension.

"I don't have one." Shy barked back in annoyance. She was done trying to convince him she wasn't the enemy. He knew she wasn't.

"Where were you going?" he demanded.

Shy turned to frown at him, "It's really none of your business."

"Careful Shy," he warned dangerously, "you know not where you tread."

She turned her face back to the window. "I'm not staying at StoneCrow. You can just tell me what it is you want and take me back to the city."

"You're coming home." The reply, made quickly, brooked no refusal.

"StoneCrow is *not* my home."

"It is now."

The statement sent a chill of foreboding washing over her.

Shy thought long and hard before she tried to appeal to his sense of decency…if he had any. "You know making me upset isn't good for the baby."

That caught his attention. His head turned to her before his eyes slid to her belly, his nostrils flaring. "I'm sorry."

The words, nearly a whisper had Shy turning to stare at him in shock. *He actually knows how to apologize?*

"I don't want to hurt the baby."

Shy clamped her mouth shut and turned sad eyes back to the window. "Yeah, just me. I get it."

"Not you either." Leto countered angrily.

"Well that's a change," she responded sarcastically and received a low warning growl in return. She frowned at him, "So what's the plan, hold me prisoner until I have my baby? What then?"

"*My* baby," he amended.

"If you think…" she'd been about to challenge his claim to her child when something pinked off the car. She silenced to listen for the noise but forgot it as soon as Leto's hand wrapped around the back of her neck and forced her to bend down seconds before the vehicle swerved violently. Gasping, she reached for the dash with one hand while the other clamped to the seat. "What's wrong?" She turned to Leto and instantly recognized the rage that tensed his features.

He struggled to control the vehicle while reaching toward Shy. One large hand fisted in the front of her shirt and he pulled her forward off the seat. "Get down!"

She did as he commanded while blurting, "What if the car flips." She could only watch his intense gaze. His hands fisted in a white-knuckled grip on the steering wheel.

"We're under attack."

Chapter 22

Attack? Oh my God! From who? She didn't need to ask, she knew. The Megalya had successfully impregnated her with a Walker child. They'd go to any lengths to re-capture her. It all made sense now that she knew that Walkers were real. It explained why the technicians had begun feeding her more and beating her less the last few weeks she'd been at Megalya, they'd known she was pregnant.

Leto too seemed to know their intent. "They won't get our baby. The Sentries are coming. Hang on Shy!"

Not knowing if he meant figuratively or literally, she braced her hands on the underside of the glove box and ducked her head. More sharp pings rang in the interior and she heard the distinctive sound of thick glass as it began to fissure.

"Leto?" Panic laced her tone. She didn't want to go back to the Megalya and she was equally as terrified of them getting their hands on Leto. She'd witnessed firsthand the torture he'd endured at their hands. She too was familiar with their viciousness. They couldn't go back. A sob escaped her when she thought of her son being subjected to them.

"I won't let them take you Shy!"

Her mind worked frantically. If they were able to stop the car, Leto would surely fight to the death to protect her and their child, but then what? She and the baby would be defenseless left to the twisted machinations of the Megalya. She knew she'd never survive their torture a second time and she certainly had no intentions of allowing them to do to her child what they'd done to her and Leto, but she couldn't allow Leto to be tortured again either.

"Shift!"

"I'm going as fast as I can," he growled through clenched teeth, his eyes riveted on the road.

"No. Shift and leave. Fly away!"

"What?" Shock was evident on his features as he ripped his gaze from the road long enough to pin her with a dazed expression.

She remembered seeing Leto strapped down in the exam room at Megalya. She hadn't been able to help him then but by God she'd help him now. "Turn into a bird and fly away Leto." Her tone was imploring, "There's no reason for them to take us all."

Leto's shock quickly dissipated as rage contorted his features. He clamped his jaw so tightly together that Shy could hear his teeth creak. "You think I'd leave you and my unborn child defenseless?"

One hand clamped over her belly, Shy lifted tear-filled eyes to stare at him, "I won't let them have my son."

Leto's enraged expression instantly softened. "Son?" The word was barely a whisper.

The world seemed to stop for a fraction of a second as she stared up at him and remembered that Jenny hadn't told him the sex of their child. All was silent as they simply stared at each other and she swore that for just a second she saw the corners of his lips lift in awe. Then the noise came and her world was turned upside down.

Her shoulder was slammed up under the dash as Leto turned his head back to the road. A vicious snarl left his lips and Shy could only watch in horror as he threw his hands up to brace against the ceiling of the car as it was jolted savagely onto its side then onto its roof.

Her own body was flung mercilessly back and forth. Banging hard against the underside of the dash before her body was slammed against the seat. She too lifted hands to brace herself when her body suddenly felt weightless and her belly heaved when she began to fall.

It all happened so quickly, in the space of one breathe, but it seemed to last forever. Glass shattered and rained onto her even as sparks flew and the sound of scraping metal could be heard. Then everything was quiet and still.

Shy opened her eyes without even realizing she'd slammed them shut. "Leto?" Her voice didn't even sound like her own, it was weak and breathy. She struggled to free herself from where she was huddled in a tight ball on the ceiling of the overturned vehicle.

Her body hurt, she felt battered. Her ribs ached where they'd slammed into the seat and one of her wrists wasn't working after it had bore the brunt of her weight as she'd tried to prevent herself from landing on her head when the vehicle flipped. Luckily, her belly felt fine. She rubbed her working hand over her abdomen and felt no pain.

"Leto!" she urged more loudly, but there was no response. It was dark and cold. She noticed that she was now able to see her breath inside the car as most of the windows had been shattered.

Righting herself, she crawled through broken glass, not caring when her good hand began to sting with multiple tiny incisions. "Leto?" She was near hysterical now. *Why isn't he answering?* Inching forward she brushed his bulk with her forearm. Blindly, she felt for him and realized his body was twisted into a huddled mass. Half trapped under the steering wheel, he was partially hung upside down while his arms hung limply over his head.

"Shit! Leto!" She felt for his chest and placed a hand there to see if he still breathed. Unfortunately, her hand was shaking too badly for her to be certain whether or not she'd actually felt any movement.

Inching closer she brushed her hand across his face and touched trembling fingers to his lips then held her breath. When her fingers warmed with damp heat she whimpered. *He's alive!* Relief swamped her only to instantly be tamped down when she heard footfall crunching over the broken glass outside the car. It was getting closer and as she strained to listen she realized it was more than one set of feet.

"Leto," she pressed her lips close to his ear, "please wake up!"

When he didn't move she was torn between trying to flee to protect their child or staying and attempting to defend his lifeless form.

The sound of footsteps halted and she crouched on all fours waiting. She turned to look behind her and was met by an angry face, which evoked a shrill shriek.

The male peered at her then let his eyes slide to Leto before shouting, "She's alive. Looks like the Walker's dead."

Next to her, somebody tried to open the passenger side door. Shy screamed and inched closer to Leto. Even unconscious, she felt safer near him.

"Fucking door's jammed," someone yelled. "Come outta there!"

Curling her body closer to Leto's, her voice quivered, "N-no!"

She heard another strange sound as her ears strained to take in their attacker's actions. She turned towards the driver's side window. Around Leto's massive frame, a dark figure held a shadowy object that she couldn't make out pointed at Leto.

"Get out now, before I put a bullet in your boyfriend!"

"I thought you said he was dead!"

"Nah," the stranger answered his friend, "there's breath coming out. He's alive…for now!" He turned his attention back to Shy, "Move bitch!"

Her fearful eyes darted to Leto. He was still unconscious and unable to tell her what to do. She wanted to protect her baby, but knew they'd shoot Leto to get her out. Then what? She'd have to come out eventually. Her good hand snaked out and rubbed Leto's cheek. She didn't want him hurt either. Slowly, she inched toward the passenger side door.

"I got her."

Before she could react rough hands grabbed her through the front windshield. She screamed as she was jerked free of the rubble. Pain seared the back of one shoulder where the jagged glass tore through her thin shirt and cut deeply into her. Sucking in another breath to scream, she swallowed it down when she heard Leto moan. She desperately wanted to call to him, but knew he'd only try to save her and the baby if he managed to break free of the vehicle. *They'll kill him!* Sealing her lips tightly, she tried to remain quiet when she was jerked to her feet.

It took a moment for her eyes to adjust, and when they did she took in the sight of five men circled around the upside down car. Each man carried a gun and all of them were pointed at the vehicle.

She turned when one man asked, "Is it her?"

The man closest to her grabbed her jaw and jerked her head to look at him. “Yeah, it’s her.” There was triumph in his voice, “The Doc’ll be pleased.”

Doc? Dr. Chambers! Oh God no! Shy eyed her surroundings, looking for a way to escape. Leto said the Sentries were coming. She could stall. She took a step back, “Y-you have the wrong people.”

A hand fisted in her hair and jerked her back into something hard. “Don’t move! And don’t waste your breath.” A crumpled photo was held up in front of her face. She had to blink back tears to see the image clearly. It was the photo of her taken at Megalya, the one they’d used on her ID. *Shit!*

“Get her in the car.”

She screamed when the hand in her hair fisted tighter and jerked her backward.

“What about him?”

“Bring him. Doc says their conception might be unique and only work with each other. If that’s the case, we’ll need him too.”

Shy had her good hand clamped around that of her captor, she was trying to keep pace with him to stop the painful tearing of her hair from her scalp. She eyed the sky hoping for some sign of the Walkers. There was none.

"Get in!"

Chapter 23

Shy was jerked back hard and shoved sideways. Falling forward, she had to land on her chest when her wounded hand failed to move to offer any support while the other remained clamped at the back of her head. Her cheek burned as she was pushed face first onto the bench seat of what she assumed was a car. Too low to be a truck, the vehicle smelled of cigarettes and alcohol.

Using a shoulder to try and right herself, hands grabbed her again and pulled her to a sitting position. A door closed and she finally got a good look at the asshole who'd been manhandling her.

Sharp beady eyes over a beak nose sat atop a sour mouth. "What the fuck you looking at?" His hand fisted in the front of her shirt and she was jerked hard into the man's chest.

The door next to her opened and a second body squeezed in on the other side of her after yelling, "Bobby! Let's go." Settling beside her the man snorted as he turned toward her, "Shit Tanner, couldn't wait for a kiss huh?"

"Bitch is staring!" When he spoke, Shy tried not to wince at his foul breath.

Another door closed and the vehicle roared to life. Her eyes left those of Tanner as she looked out his window to see the other two men carrying Leto from the demolished vehicle.

"Wait!"

Tanner clawed a hand over her face, "Don't worry. He's coming!"

As the vehicle sped away, a sinking feeling settled over her. If they'd kept them together at least she'd have been sure that Leto was okay.

"Aren't they worried he'll wake up? Maybe you shoulda stayed Tanner."

Tanner released her face and shirt and sat back in his seat. "They'll be fine. The freak is going in the trunk."

Trunk? Oh God, he'll freeze! Shy wanted to speak up but knew she'd only be abused further, and it's not like anyone cared what she had to say anyway. Instead, she prayed that wherever they were taking her and Leto it wasn't too far. When night had fallen so had the temperature, and if Leto didn't wake and shift she was certain he'd freeze to death in the trunk.

The man to her left pulled out a cell phone and dialed before holding it up to his ear. "It's Casey. We got her!"

There was silence in the car then, "We got him too! Alive. We're en route now." Then he hung up and shouted, "Hooeee! I can't believe we got him too! Shit boys, that triples our pay day!"

Shy stared straight ahead trying to determine where they were headed.

Casey turned to smile at her, "Do you have any idea how much you're worth?"

She refused to look at him and remained silent with her eyes forward.

"I think we should pull over and have a little fun." Tanner's foul breath filled the backseat as he spoke.

"Not happening." Casey sobered, "If she's injured in any way we lose half. That was the deal."

Tanner leaned forward to frown around her, "She's already injured. Her wrist is broke. You think we won't get docked for that?" He fell back against the seat, "I'm just saying if we're gonna lose half, we might as well get some enjoyment out of it too."

Shy fought to keep from retching. The thought of Tanner touching any part of her was repulsive. Silently she prayed that Casey stood his ground.

"We're not getting docked for her wrist. Doc is concerned about the baby. That means no fucking her."

Tanner leaned forward again, "We could fuck her in the ass."

Shy stiffened and curled the fingers of her good hand into a tight fist. She'd fight to the death to keep them from touching her in that manner.

The driver started laughing and his eyes found Tanner's in the rearview mirror. "Jeez bro, get laid much? Shit! You act like you haven't had any in a year."

Tanner sat back again but Shy could feel him tense. He was angry. "Fuck you Bobby!"

Bobby started laughing again, “Sounds like you’d actually like to!”

Both Bobby and Casey erupted into laughter. When Casey sobered he rubbed at his eyes, “When we get paid you can buy all the pussy you want. For now, hands off.”

They drove in silence for what felt like an eternity before Casey turned to nod at Tanner.

Tanner grabbed her around the neck and forced her head down into his lap. She tried to pull back but he only pushed harder.

“Sorry sweets,” it was Casey’s voice, “but you can’t see where we’re going.”

She tried to struggle free, but with only one good hand she couldn’t gain any leverage to shove out of Tanner’s lap. When his grasp on the back of her neck became brutal, she stilled and allowed him to hold her down.

He rubbed her face against his groin and she gagged when she felt the unmistakable ridge of his erection as he rubbed her cheek back and forth over the denim.

She heard Casey laugh, "Well I suppose that's acceptable."

Shy tried to push away but only succeeded in being forced harder against Tanner's lap. She heard him moan and then growl, "You're gonna suck it bitch!"

The knuckles of his free hand brushed her cheek as he tried to unbutton his pants.

"Don't do that man!" Casey sounded horrified, "Do you honestly trust her not to bite?"

Tanner's finger's stilled and then were gone.

"We're here anyway."

Tanner stopped rubbing and she felt the car ease to a halt.

She was jerked back to a sitting position and watched as Bobby climbed from the car followed by Casey. "We'll make sure the coast is clear. When I signal, bring her to the van."

Terrified to be left alone with Tanner, Shy tried to inch her body away from his. He grabbed her arm and jerked her out of the car. Before she could even get her balance she was shoved back against the car. Her lower back exploded in pain when she was thrown against the protruding door handle. Tanner's body crushed into hers as he smiled menacingly revealing that he was missing several teeth.

His hand slid up and wrapped tightly around her throat while the other dropped out of her line of vision. She heard the rustling of clothes then the sound of a zipper. She lifted her good hand trying to force his hand from her throat to jerk back, but his hold on her throat tightened.

"Don't worry bitch, I won't fuck you. But that doesn't mean there aren't other ways to get off."

His hand caught her wrist and rubbed her hand down his chest forcing it lower until he held it over his hard cock.

Terror quickly turned to revulsion before Shy let her fingers curl. Her nails dug into tender flesh as she slowly added pressure.

Tanner's smile vanished and his eyes widened when she clamped her hand onto his man hood and clawed as hard as she could, letting her nails dig into flesh.

He howled in pain before pulling back an arm and punching her hard in the face.

Shy reeled, but luckily she'd turned her head at the last moment taking the punch high on her cheek bone. It hurt, but not as bad as it would have if he'd connected with her nose.

Shy's hand clutched at her cheek and she ignored Tanner as he dropped to the ground and writhed in pain as he attempted to zip his pants. A low rumbling in the trees behind the car had both her and Tanner snapping their heads in the direction of the sound.

Tanner scrambled to his feet and Shy took a chance. Before he could reach for her she raced toward the tree line. She wasn't fast, but didn't need to be. She felt Tanner grab the back of her shirt and she ducked her head and crashed to her knees when a mountain lion vaulted over her head and slammed Tanner back against the ground.

Shy prayed the beast was a Walker but didn't stick around to find out. She ran!

Vicious snarls rent the air behind her and lent strength to her legs as she dashed between trees, using her good hand to clamp her broken wrist against her body. She jumped over a stump and the jarring pain to her wrist had her clamping her teeth together even as her fear ebbed a fraction and anger bubbled to the surface. She was tired of running, tired of being the victim. What she'd already endured should have been enough! She thought of the Skin Walkers and their existence and felt a swell of pity knowing that her life for the last half a year was how they'd had to live their entire lives. It wasn't fair.

Lost in thought, Shy nearly collided with the massive body that stepped into the path in front of her. Her feet slid in the pine needle covered earth and she recoiled when the man reached for her. She slipped but scrambled backward as best she could, her eyes round with fear.

She'd hoped he was a Walker, a friend, but when he stepped from the shadows into the light Shy didn't recognize him. When he bent to reach for her again she did the only thing she had left. The terrified scream was ripped from her throat as she fought the man who clamped strong hands onto her arms.

"LETOOOOOOO!"

The man was hauling her up from the ground when a flash of fur took him down and had Shy falling back to land hard on her ass.

The large man fought with the mountain lion and Shy, who'd been about to make a run for it, froze in place when she heard numerous foot-steps pounding toward them. Her head whipped around when someone stopped behind her. Tears of relief filled her eyes when York dropped to a knee and pulled her into his arms.

"LETO! REDKNIFE! STOP!"

Shy recognized Conn's voice, but didn't look up. The snarls and grunts of the fighting stopped and she felt York tense around her.

"Let go of her!"

Leto's voice above her had her pulling back from York's arms even as they tightened around her.

"You failed to protect her!" York's tone was accusatory and challenging.

"YORK!"

Both men looked at Conn and Shy took advantage of the opportunity to scramble to her feet. She backed away from the two men as they squared off.

"You never wanted her Leto. Give her to me."

What? Shy paled and backed up some more.

Leto's head lowered as his upper lip curled back in a fierce snarl to reveal elongated canines. "Never!"

"Shy?" Conn ignored Leto and York and inched closer to her.

A soft whimper escaped her parted lips and it drew the attention of both Leto and York. Concern flashed across both men's features and they advanced.

"DON'T!" Shy held up her good hand and when she took a step back her knees buckled. It was all just too much.

"Shit!" All three men lunged for her, but Conn was the one to catch her before she could hit the ground.

"Give her to me!" Leto growled.

Obviously displeased, Conn looked from Leto to York in apparent indecision before holding Shy's slumped form out and allowing her Walker to take her.

Chapter 24

Leto was livid. How dare York attempt to claim what was his. Shy carried his child and his scent and still the Celtic Walker had the audacity to ask Leto to relinquish her. Looking up he glared across the Hummer at the red-haired Walker that still watched him as if he intended on hurting his angel. A low warning growl vibrated in his chest.

"Knock it off Leto!" Conn peered back from the driver's seat and flashed sad eyes to York. "She's safe. It's all that matters."

"She would never have been placed in danger if she were mine!"

Leto wished he could set Shy down and beat seven shades of shit out of York. The man was basically accusing him of failing to protect his mate. Hell, he hadn't even been at StoneCrow when she'd escaped. He and the Chief of Security, King Mulholland, had left as soon as he'd carried Shy to the infirmary and been assured she and his baby were safe.

After watching the video of what had happened to Shy, he'd felt sickened. Not only had he assumed too much, he'd been flat out fucking wrong. She'd suffered as he had…worse! He'd caught her when she'd fainted and felt sheer terror seize him when Monroe, who Leto had never seen get emotional, paled and ordered Leto to get Shy to the infirmary. Wordlessly, Leto had stalked to the door when Monroe shoved him and barked, "Run Leto! She's with child…*your* child."

A million questions had raced through his mind but he didn't stall to ask. Instead he tore down the hallway and raced to the first floor infirmary, cursing that the CEO's office was on the third floor.

When he arrived at the infirmary Jenny was waiting for them.

"Lay her here!"

The Doctor had made short work of attaching monitors and checking Shy's vitals. She smeared a lubricant on Shy's too flat belly and scanned her with some device.

Whoosh-whoosh, whoosh-whoosh, whoosh-whoosh.

The sound startled Leto and he gaped at Jenny.

Her eyes found his and she frowned. "It's your baby's heart. The child is under stress." She pulled the device away and the rapid sound stopped. "What in the hell were you idiots doing up there?"

Unable to formulate any words, Leto shook his head as shame seared him. He hadn't known…the information was too much.

Jenny drew in a deep breath and exhaled slowly, struggling to regain her composure. Her angry expression softened. "She was artificially inseminated by the Megalya. It's why they held her. It's why she carries your scent. She carries your child."

For the first time in his life, Leto felt the sting of tears at the back of his eyes. *I'm going to have a child with…* His eyes flashed to Shy and he knew in that moment beyond any shadow of a doubt that Shy was his angel.

Tearing his furious gaze from York and his memories, Leto looked down at the fragile creature passed out in his arms. Her face was pale but she was breathing evenly. There was a dark bruise and swelling under one of her eyes and high on her cheek and her wrist was the size of an orange. Knowing he'd killed the Megalya lackeys quite painfully did little to placate his anger.

Shy stirred and Leto lifted her higher so that her head was propped against his shoulder, her lips brushing his neck. One strong arm wrapped around her shoulders and a possessive hand clamped on her thigh. He looked up and caught York frowning at his hand on Shy's thigh and just to piss the other Walker off, he inched it higher until it curved possessively over her rounded hip.

York's head snapped up, his eyes locking with Leto's. God he wanted to kill York! He wanted to rip the Walker limb from fucking limb and if the Walker continued to look at his Shy as if *he* had some claim to her than that's exactly what Leto intended to do.

"ETA four minutes. Jenny's waiting so be ready."

Even in her unconscious state Leto could scent Shy's pain. It had been the same when, after watching the video of her being tortured and she'd passed out, he'd carried her to the infirmary. Emotional pain and physical pain smelled different, but when either scent emanated from Shy it put Leto into a killing rage. It's why he'd left her in the infirmary and gone hunting. He wanted to kill every single technician he'd seen on the video and it wasn't a fantasy. He'd do it if it was the last thing he ever did. He'd get Shy to safety, get her home, get her healed, and then get back out there to avenge his angel, his mate!

When he'd decided she was his, he didn't know. When Monroe had told him she was pregnant with his child he'd been overwhelmed simultaneously by fear for Shy and the baby, regret over his treatment of her, and more fucking joy than he ever thought possible. Deep down he realized that a part of him had known she was his all along. It's why he'd never been able to harm her even when he knew she was an admitted Megalya. Guilt ate at him over his treatment of her. If he'd known then...

He couldn't beat himself up over it. All he could do was protect her now. He slid his hand from her hip and placed it gently over her belly and his child that grew within. Without moving his head his eyes snapped up to sneer at York who still watched him intently. "MINE!" he growled with such a fierce possession and vehemence that he knew it wasn't just for show. Shy belonged to him. She was his angel and the first chance he got he intended to bind her and claim her!

***

Shy woke back in the infirmary and moaned at both the ache in her muscles and cheek as well as the throbbing in her wrist. Looking up she was surprised to find Leto standing over her with concern marring his handsome features.

Memory came back and her hand flashed to her belly. "The baby?"

Leto twined strong fingers with hers, "He's fine. It's you I'm worried about. I can scent her pain." He looked up and Shy followed his gaze to Dr. Jenny Arkinson.

"Well," Jenny began reluctantly, "we can't give her a very strong pain reliever due to the baby, and the mild shot that I did give her has already been burned off by her accelerated metabolism." Her perfectly manicured brows furrowed, "Carrying a Walker child isn't the same as carrying a fully human child Leto. The gestation period is more rapid. Shy will need to eat more frequently, sleep more often. She's in an incredibly fragile state right now." Jenny turned sad eyes to Shy, "Unfortunately, we have had few Walker children born here at StoneCrow and all of those have been female. Your son is a miracle and a very terrifying one for me to have to deal with. This is a case of first impression for me."

Shy looked to Leto with worried eyes before staring back at Jenny.

"I'm assuming that because Walker men are stronger that your son will demand more from your body Shy. This is going to be difficult for you. Honestly, I'd like to admit you for the duration of the pregnancy but Leto has already refused."

Shocked, Shy looked at Leto. She agreed with him. There was no way in hell she'd be confined to a bed for the next nine or so months...*wait!* "What do you mean the gestation period is more rapid?"

"Mahkya Mulholland, King and Lilly's daughter, was born at just seven months. I believe your son will come sooner."

Shy gasped and struggled to sit up, "Sooner?"

Leto reached down and gently eased her to a sitting position as Shy noted her swollen wrist was now wrapped in a bulky brace.

"How much sooner?"

Jenny shrugged, "I'm not sure. Hopefully around six or more preferably five months."

"Hopefully?" She felt fear inch up her spine.

Shaking her head Jenny threw her hands up in a resignation. "Look, your heart rate has increased with the baby's demand for blood supply. That coupled with your increased need for food and rest. It's putting a strain on your system that will only increase as your son grows. Carrying this child to term could be…" She dropped her gaze.

"Fatal?" Shy supplied shakily.

Leveling her eyes first on Shy then on Leto, Jenny nodded once. "Potentially, yes." She cleared her throat and Shy saw the intent as she began, "Perhaps it might be best if we just…"

"NO!" Shy refused to let her finish.

"You need to hear me out," Jenny demanded.

Confused, Leto looked from Jenny to Shy.

"No Jenny! It's not an option. Don't suggest it; don't even waste your breath."

Realization dawned and Leto growled. "I have no say?"

"No!" Shy snapped swinging her legs around off the med bed. "You don't."

Both Dr. Arkinson and Leto were shocked by Shy's outburst.

"As a matter of fact, you can leave."

"It's my child Shy."

"Wrong," she countered, "it's *my* child. You hate me remember." Slowly she inched off the table and stood on wobbly legs. When Leto reached for her she slapped his hands away. "You finally know the truth and must now know that you have no cause to hate me or hunt me or…*harm* me." She walked toward the door. "I'd appreciate it if you'd leave me alone."

Turning at the door, she caught Jenny attempting to hide a smile while a look of such distressing exclusion crossed Leto's face that she actually felt bad. The look only lasted a moment before his brows furrowed and he crossed the room in seconds. Two strong hands gripped her hips and he lifted her, forcing himself between her legs and shelving her ass with one arm so that she was wrapped around him as he carried her back to the med bed.

"Hey! Put me down." As Leto walked, he pulled Shy into him and the friction caused when he walked had her clenching her teeth at the luscious sensation of her sex rubbing up against him.

"Don't get riled up Shy," Jenny ordered, "it's not good for the baby. Besides, you do need to hang on for just a moment; I've got some meds I need to retrieve for you and then I'll get you signed out."

"Fine," she crossed her arms over her chest and tried to ignore the zing of interest that shot through her when Leto had wrapped her around him. Her breasts felt instantly swollen and she wasn't crossing her arms in an attempt to appear formidable but rather to hide her nipples that had instantly pebbled and hardened to stiff peaks as they'd rubbed against Leto's chest as he'd walked with her.

It's the pregnancy, she lied trying to convince herself that her sudden flat out horniness was hormonal and had nothing to do with the Walker whose child she carried.

Jenny exited the room while Leto towered over her with his body still between her legs as she sat on the bed. She tried not to look at him as she fought her own arousal. God he was hot. Her eyes locked on his broad well-defined chest and slid down his thickly corded arms to rest on his hands. She remembered the way he'd touched her, how he'd made her come. Her sex creamed with wanting and when Leto inhaled loudly and a long deep rumble emitted from his chest, Shy's horrified gaze shot up.

His eyes had darkened dangerously and she recognized the burning desire that reflected in the swirling brown and black depths.

She was in trouble. Serious, serious trouble! When he'd hated her she hadn't even considered him but now that he knew the truth, now that he was protecting her and was telling York that she was his! Shy shifted uncomfortably as she dropped her eyes. She knew he could scent a lie and from his reaction just now, she knew he'd scented her arousal. She reached down and planted her good hand on the side of her hips as she attempted to shimmy back. She wanted him away from her so she could at least clamp her thighs together in an effort to stifle some of her feminine heat.

Instead, strong hands clamped on her thighs and held her in place. Too afraid to look up she opted to chew on her bottom lip nervously as she waited for Jenny to return.

Long minutes passed and Leto slid his hands an inch or so higher. Shy's body reacted. Her clit literally throbbed demanding attention and she sucked in a sharp breath. He slid his hands up another inch or so until his thumbs buried themselves in the bend of her hips. Her heart thundered in response. She had to put a stop to this. "Don't!" Her voice sounded breathy and weak even to her own ears.

"Look at me!" Leto demanded.

Shy slowly lifted her eyes and felt her sexual juices gather at the look of pure lust on his handsome face. "W-what?" Her voice sounded tellingly husky.

He simply stared at her for long moments before his brows speared down in his typical scowl. "I'm sorry Shy."

She was dazed by his apology. He had a lot to be sorry for but it didn't keep her from asking, "For what?"

"For not seeing what you are."

A pink tongue darted out to wet her dry lips. "And what am I Leto?"

He didn't hesitate. "You are mine."

Chapter 25

Jenny entered before Shy could ask what Leto meant when he said she was his. She knew she blushed when Jenny's lips tweaked.

"So, here are some mild pain killers for your wrist."

"Did you get the information I asked about?"

Shy tried to ignore Leto as he impatiently grilled the doctor.

"Yes," Jenny spoke through clenched teeth, "but perhaps you could simply ask her."

That drew Shy's attention. She scowled up at Leto. "Ask who what?"

Ignoring her, Leto's gaze narrowed on Jenny, "You're sure it's safe?"

"Yes," Jenny bit out bracing her hands on her hips in a show of disapproval. "But as I said, you might want to…"

He didn't hesitate to reach up and jerk his halo free. Shy watched curiously as it seared the flesh around Leto's throat, branding him upon its removal before he thrust it forward. She jumped when it locked in place around her slender throat but then the strength melted from her body and when she made to blink her eyes didn't reopen.

Smiling, Leto scooped an unconscious Shy into his arms and smiled at Jenny.

"…ask her." Jenny finished on an exasperated sigh.

"Mine," Leto growled.

"Yes, I know Tarzan." Jenny pointed to the door. "Go! Claim! Assert your dominance!" She turned and shook her head while muttering, "Damn possessive Walker men."

Leto stalked from the infirmary with his angel cradled in his arms. He couldn't stop smiling. *Mine! My angel! With my child!* He'd never had anyone before and the pride he'd felt at knowing Shy carried his child was only multiplied by the fact that he'd just gifted her with his halo. The knowledge that no one could remove it, not even Shy, had him giddy with such a sense of eager anticipation he could barely contain it. She was his…forever!

***

Shy woke coming. She squeezed her eyes tighter closed as she slowly became aware. Fighting to stay asleep and ride out the last tendrils of the orgasm that wrapped deliciously around her she clenched her thighs tighter together and licked her lips at the glorious sensation it evoked when the material of her panties pressed against her swollen clit and shot pure rapture straight to her womb.

Slowly, memories forced their way to the surface and reality set in. Her eyes snapped open and she was shocked and humiliated to find Leto leaning over her with an ear-to-ear grin on his face.

Does he know? She tried to control her erratic breathing.

"You smell so good when you're wet."

Yep he knows! She felt her cheeks singe so brightly that it actually stung.

Leto licked his lips and a growl emitted from his chest as his eyes darkened with hunger. "Say I can have a taste Shy." His voice was deeper than normal, animalistic, and pained.

Taste? Oh God... She clenched her thighs tighter together as her pussy spasmed at the mere thought of Leto's tongue sliding through her now drenched folds. Her nipples were hardened and ached where they rubbed against the fabric of her shirt. Looking down she realized two things. One, she was on a bed in a large room and two, she was still fully clothed.

"How did you?" She stared at him accusingly, "Did you touch me while I was asleep?" She tried to sit up but Leto moved too quickly. Using a knee, he spread her legs and settled his body between them until his chest was pressed into hers.

"I would not touch you without permission."

"Then how did you?" Her cheeks flamed again and she was too embarrassed to finish the question.

She didn't have to. Leto smiled knowingly and his eyes dipped to her throat. "Your halo."

Halo? Lifting a hand she grabbed the stiff band that was clasped around her throat. Her tone was accusatory, "What did you do to me?"

"I bound you Shy. You are mine!"

She tried to wiggle out from under him but stilled when Leto threw his head back and moaned in pleasure. She felt the nudge of his erect cock as it pressed into her sex and she swallowed at the wave of desire that crashed over her. "Y-you bound me and I…reacted?" She was confused, the Walker jargon made no sense to her.

Lowering his head, Leto's expression looked tense. "No. Your pleasure was evoked."

"I thought you said you didn't touch me," she challenged.

"I didn't." His eyes twinkled mischievously, "I can show you what I did."

Shy's mind raced. *If he didn't touch me than how did he…* Confident that because she was awake and could thwart his advances he wouldn't be able to provoke such a response again, Shy nodded once. It was a mistake.

Leto's smile faded and she felt a rumble in his chest as he lowered his head toward her throat.

Shy stiffened, "I thought you didn't touch me!"

He pulled back a fraction to frown at her. "I didn't. Tilt your head."

She stared at him for a few moments before tilting her head and exposing her neck. *Is he going to bite me?*

One of his hands reached up and gripped her around the back of the neck holding her in place. Fear shot through her. *He could still hate me! This could all be a ruse.* "Leto?" Fear made her voice tremble.

He growled but didn't pull back as his breath fanned her throat, "Don't move. I would never harm you. You are mine. I would rather die than to see you hurt Shy."

Well that was new. Her heart thundered in her chest as he lowered his head and she pinched her eyes shut and waited for him to sink his teeth into her. It never happened. Instead, ecstasy tore through her. Her hips bucked involuntarily and she couldn't hold back the wanton gasp that escaped her parted lips.

Confusion hit hard. Leto was pressed against her, his hips weren't moving, and the only place they touched skin to skin was where he held the back of her neck. She sucked in a breath to ask what was happening when her pussy creamed and spilled its juices as she felt satiny bliss whisper over her clit. Her back arched and her swollen breasts ached to be suckled.

Blindly she forced her good hand between their bodies. Leto lifted his hips to allow her to feel the vee between her legs. She was still fully clothed. She didn't…

Ribbons of ecstasy unfurled in her limbs and if her hand wasn't there to ensure it she would have believed that Leto's face was buried between her thighs. Near her ear she heard the soft smacking of his wet tongue and she fought to focus on what it was exactly he was doing, but whatever it was, it was too much. She felt his tongue brush her neck and when it wrapped around the halo at her throat Shy swore it breached her pussy and sent her over the edge. She screamed his name when the orgasm gripped her. The fingers peeking out from her brace clawed at his shoulder and the other firmly gripped his hip as the spasms rocked her body until they became only a slight flutter.

Her body melted into the mattress as her heated muscles finally relaxed. Leto had made her come…*twice*…just by licking her halo. *God if he's tongue can do that to me up there just imagine...*

She didn't have to. Leto pulled back with a snarl and his hands went to the front of her jeans. He ripped them open and had her pants and drenched panties off and flung across the room before she could come to her senses.

She reached down to cover herself, "Stop! What are you doing?"

Leto snarled at the hand that covered his target. Shy noted that his canines had elongated and his eyes were pure black. It was both erotic and terrifying.

"You are mine! Move your hand so I can claim you."

Shy scrambled to get away from him, but one hand locked solidly around her ankle and jerked her back to him. He dropped as he pulled her close so that her thighs were braced on each of his shoulders and his breath blew hot against the hand that still covered her bare sex. To her mortification Leto inhaled deeply and what sounded like a purr rumbled from his chest.

"Leto, no! We can't!"

His eyes shot up from between her legs to narrow on her, "Why? You are mine!"

"W-what? No. I'm not... Stop...saying *that*!"

He titled his head sideways, "You are punishing me for my mistreatment of you."

Shocked Shy shook her head. "No, I wouldn't use sex like that. I just...we just met. I don't even know you."

"I am your Walker," he stated angrily. "You carry my child. You wear my halo. You are mine Shy. I would die for you and for our child."

She tried to lift her thighs from his shoulders but stopped when he loosed a vicious growl. "This is all too fast. I don't know what any of this means." Tears flooded her eyes, "Last week you hated me. You wanted Monroe to lock me up. Y-you wanted me *dead*."

His expression softened. "I was wrong. I apologize."

"*A-apologize!*" she gasped, incredulity lacing her tone. "You can't just apologize for something like that. I lost months of my life because of you and you wanted me killed for it, and now you just *apologize*?"

"I see now that I hurt you. I can give you time Shy, but it won't be long." His eyes dipped to the hand that covered her pussy, "I ache to be inside you." He dipped his head and nudged her fingers with his nose. The hand didn't move so he placated himself with licking the juices from the insides of her thighs. When he looked up his features were strained, "You taste like home. Inside you is where I belong."

He shot up from the bed and Shy's eyes dropped to where his sweats were tented by his huge erection.

"When you are ready to…claim me," the words seemed forced, "let me know. Until then you are not to leave this cabin or my sight. I will kill any man that touches you Shy. I won't be able to control it. The men here are my friends, but it wouldn't matter to me. Please keep that in mind." Then he turned and exited the room slamming the door behind him before Shy heard a shower blast on somewhere in the small cabin.

Chapter 26

If Shy thought before that she was doomed, she *knew* so now. The Leto that had looked upon her with undisguised hatred and mistrust was difficult to bear but he was nothing compared to the Leto that had chased her down, protected her, kept claiming that she was his, and professed his willingness to die in order to protect her and their unborn child. Where before he wanted her gone from StoneCrow, now there was no hope of ever escaping, not alone, and certainly not with their son.

It had only been a day since Leto had brought her to his cabin and he seemed to grow restless by the hour. The night before he'd returned and had forced her to sleep in his arms. He'd claimed it was for her safety but she doubted any man or Walker alive would confront Leto in his now obsessive state.

He'd fed her often, too often and when she wasn't eating she was forced to lie in bed. After breakfast he'd carried her from the kitchen back to his bed. Shy had argued that she wasn't sleepy but Leto demanded that she rest. Staring up at the ceiling she flinched when her belly growled. It had only been about two hours since she'd eaten a large breakfast of buttery pancakes, scrambled eggs, bacon, and freshly squeezed orange juice. *No way!*

There was no way she was going to let Leto force feed her, she didn't care how much her belly growled. It just didn't make sense that she could be hungry again so soon after breakfast.

As if on cue, the bedroom door opened and Leto silently stalked to the bed and bent to scoop her into his arms.

"Don't!" She struggled to get to her feet. "I'm not hungry and I *can* walk ya' know*!*" Her belly growled and her face flamed when Leto smiled and nodded once as if that settled the matter. He picked her up and she could only cross her arms over her chest like a petulant child.

"Leto put me down. I'm not hungry. There's no way I can be. I just ate enough for an army about two-seconds ago."

He didn't even look at her as he strode effortlessly to the kitchen. "The baby wants food."

"Well I don't!" She knew how selfish it sounded but if Leto had his way she'd be four-hundred pounds by the time the baby was born. "I want to go for a walk…*outside!*"

He didn't even look at her. "No. Eat." He shoved a plate holding a sandwich and a pile of potato chips in front of her then stalked to the fridge and pulled out a gallon of milk.

Shy glowered at the sandwich. The stupid ham and turkey on wheat smelled delicious and had her mouth watering. She had to fight to keep from popping a potato chip into her mouth while Leto's back was turned. "I'm not eating." She re-crossed her arms over her chest.

Leto brought her a glass of milk and set it beside the plate as he dropped into the chair beside her and simply stared. "Eat."

"You eat! I haven't seen you take a single bite of anything since I've been here, but yet you have no qualms about forcing food down my throat." She'd thought about that while she'd been forced to stay in bed and part of her wondered if Walker's didn't have some strange diet. Leto looked thinner and more pale than he had the days after they'd been rescued and fattened up. He looked worn out and she wondered what was causing it. Her presence? Was he allowing her to stay with him out of guilt over the fact that she was pregnant with his child? Did he really just want her gone?

"I can't eat." The statement was simply made and had Shy sitting a little straighter as her curiosity piqued.

"Why?"

"Because you haven't claimed me yet."

"What?" Shy unfolded her arms, propping her bandaged wrist on the table.

"I am afflicted Shy. I cannot eat or sleep until you claim me."

Afflicted? She remembered Aries and Jenny speaking about it. "What is afflicted?"

He shrugged one shoulder. "It means I…" he smiled wickedly then and Shy knew she was in trouble. His eyes slid down to linger on her lips before dropping to rest on her breasts. "I need to spill my seed deep inside you to mark you as mine."

Shy felt her entire body flush. *Have I lost my damn mind?* She tried to look appalled while her body begged her to give Leto what he wanted and God did she ever want to give him what he wanted. She yearned to bask in the safety of his embrace and the demanding inferno she was certain she'd find in his lips. His gaze alone left a scorched trail wherever it skimmed her flesh. She wanted him and he wanted her and every minute they were together it was harder and harder for her to deny her attraction. Attraction hell, he'd become the object of her desire, the man of her dreams, and wasn't he already the father of her child? *What could it hurt?*

As if sensing the minute fissure in Shy's defenses Leto pressed, "You should claim me. It isn't safe for you or our baby for me to be in a weakened state. I need to be strong to protect you both."

Her eyes rounded, "Protect us from what?"

Leto's eyes swept the room and lingered on the large bay window in the living room. "From everything!"

"But Leto," she didn't get to finish.

"I'm not going anywhere Shy," he drew his eyes from the window and let them settle on her as he slid from his chair to kneel beside her, his hand finding hers and holding it to his chest. "Just as you belong to me, I belong to you. I want no one else and I'll never need anything else but this," he squeezed her hand tighter.

"You don't have to claim me now Shy, but you *will* claim me!" His voice took on a deep rumble and Shy doubted she'd ever deny him anything.

His proximity was distracting and the way his thumb rubbed over the back of her hand had her fighting to concentrate on what he was saying. Suddenly she was very hungry but it wasn't for food.

"I know I've been…off lately. I've been told it's part of the affliction. Thinking coherently, *speaking* coherently. It's difficult when all I want to do is bury my dick so deep inside your sweet pussy that neither one of us knows where the other ends and we begin."

The words sent a punch of lust straight to Shy's womb and she tried to pull her hand free but Leto merely held tighter.

"I'm consumed with you Shy, the thought of touching you, having you, claiming you, and of raising our child with you." He lowered his eyes, "And I can wait for you to forgive me. Dr. Arkinson has me on supplements and I should be okay…"

"Supplements?" Shy's brow furrowed. "What do you mean you should be okay?" She jerked her hand free and got to her feet. "Why wouldn't you be okay? What's going on?" She almost smiled when Leto growled then slowly rose to his feet, spearing an angry hand into his satiny black hair.

"I can't eat or sleep without a claiming. The halo only ties you to me. It doesn't mark you as mine. I have to do that. Nature's way of ensuring I'm not too dumb to overlook my angel is to prevent me from eating or sleeping until I claim her."

Shy's mouth fell open. "But…Leto, it's been…" she couldn't even remember how many days it had been since they'd been released. "When did it start?"

He smiled but it didn't reach his eyes, "Do you remember when I first saw you in the motel room? When you dropped me to my knees?"

"That was…"

He nodded, "That was the beginning of the affliction. The second I laid eyes on you I knew that you were mine."

Shy fought down her lust as concern overrode the emotion. "What happens if…if I don't claim you?"

His expression darkened instantly, "You'll not have anyone else." His hands locked around her arms and pulled her into him as he frowned down at her.

"No," she shook her head, "I don't *want* anyone else." She felt herself blush at the comment but carried on, "What I mean is, what happens if we wait? How long can you go on like this?"

He shrugged one shoulder, "Apparently I now hold the record. No one knows what will happen if the affliction is ignored." He smiled, "We could be the first case."

"That's not funny." Shy actually paled and it didn't go unnoticed.

"Are you ill?" Leto didn't even ask before scooping Shy up and rushing toward the bathroom.

"No, I'm not!"

Leto stopped just outside the bathroom door.

"If you're not eating and not sleeping," she shook her head. "Please take me to the bedroom."

Shy looked sick and he could scent her fear. Something was wrong with his angel. He gently placed her on the bed and pulled a blanket to cover her. "Stay! I'll get Jenny." Before he could leave, Shy's hand gripped his forearm.

The words that escaped her lips had Leto dropping to a knee beside the bed.

"I-I *claim* you Leto."

Chapter 27

Leto didn't move. He was afraid that the action would somehow shatter the spell and cause Shy to change her mind.

"Did you hear me?"

Her soft voice called to him and had him turning, his eyes narrowing on where she lay on the bed. "Say it again," he commanded, slowly getting to his feet.

"I'm not sure if I said it right or if I'm even supposed to…"

She was rambling and he could scent her discomfort and uncertainty but he knew what he'd heard. He wouldn't allow her to back out. "Say it again," he growled impatiently and regretted the fierceness of his tone when Shy sucked in her bottom lip and lifted the blanket higher under her chin with her good hand.

"I...said I claim you."

Her eyes refused to meet his and as much as he wanted to ensure she knew what she was doing, the words were enough. The blood that seemed to have stalled to a cold sludge in his veins over the past few weeks surged to life with a fiery rush that had his flesh heating and his balls swelling. His senses instantly heightened and under her insecurity and hesitation, Leto could scent Shy's heat. It wasn't lip service or pity. She wanted him!

***

Shy watched as Leto's nostrils flared. The heat that stole into his eyes had her simultaneously nervous and excited. Goosebumps rose on her flesh and when Leto's hands gripped the hem of his shirt and jerked it over his head, her eyes locked on the rock hard abs that were revealed. He drew closer but she couldn't seem to pull her eyes from where they drank in his impossible physique. Finally, when strong hands gripped the button on his jeans, Shy was able to raise her eyes to his.

He watched her intently as he slowly undid his buttons and pushed the denim over lean hips. Unsure what else to do Shy turned her head even as she felt her cheeks singe. She hadn't missed the huge erection that sprang forth and bobbed its demand for attention.

"Once we do this Shy there is no going back. You'll be mine."

She lifted her eyes and wanted to ask what he meant but he was already crawling onto the bed, gloriously naked. The sight sent a shiver of excitement coursing through her. She planted her good hand and had intended on scooting to the side to give Leto some room but his hand clamped on her thigh.

"Don't!" he growled.

"I-I wasn't leaving."

"Don't run from me Shy. Not now. I won't be able to control myself. I'll chase you and force you down to bury my dick so far inside you…"

The thought should have terrified her but as usual where this Walker was concerned, the image his words brought to life only excited her. She shook her head and promised, "I won't run."

Leto's eyes dropped to the hand on her thigh and he rubbed before his brow crinkled and he pinched the denim fabric of her jeans between his fingers. "Take this off!" He sat back on his heels and eyed her shirt. "Take it *all* off!"

Shy wasn't inexperienced with sex but getting naked in front of a practical stranger wasn't something she was comfortable doing with all the lights still on.

"Can you turn off the light?"

"No. I want to see you."

She lowered her eyes again, not wanting him to see her embarrassment. "Please Leto? This is kind of…weird."

"I'm naked," he challenged.

"I'm modest," she threw back just as quickly.

***

Leto seemed to struggle with her request before he growled and jerked back from the bed. Quickly he stomped to the light and flicked it off. He didn't bother telling Shy that he could see in the dark. Before he knelt back on the bed he felt a pang of guilt. He was moments away from claiming his Shy but it felt incomplete. All his life he'd witnessed fellow Walkers claim their angels. Typically, it was done slowly with some form of courtship. Now, he'd foolishly done just as Commander Drago had and permitted things to get too far along to allow his angel any of the wooing and flattery that was a typical precursor to a claiming. What's worse was the protocol had been forgone by his mistaken belief that she was his enemy. She wasn't getting what she deserved because of him.

"Did you change your mind?"

Shy's soft voice calling to him from the dark made him realize that he'd stopped just short of climbing onto the bed.

The bed dipped as he crawled over her, his warm body slid over the smoothness of her own and he realized that she'd stripped. He'd had intentions of asking her if she wanted to wait, if she wanted to be courted, but when his body rubbed against the satiny heat of her own his hope of waiting was lost.

He settled on his knees between her spread thighs and he felt goose bumps speckle her flesh. "Are you cold?"

"No."

He placed both hands on her slender ankles and slowly eased them up her body. His calloused hands skimmed firm thighs and rounded hips. His thumbs touched each other where her waist tapered and then drew apart again as her rib cage flared beneath his touch. When he cupped two heavy breasts, Shy shivered.

Dipping his head, he took one berry ripe nipple into his mouth. Shy arched beneath him and he felt her small nails biting into the flesh of his shoulders. The thought that she might mark him excited him and had him tugging on her nipple with greater suction even as his tongue flicked her nipple.

"Leto," Shy moaned his name and her legs bent. She pressed against him and he could feel the liquid heat of her core.

One hand left her breast to smooth down her back and over a rounded hip before he cupped her ass. He wanted to go slow, he swore to the Gods he was going to but his dick ached so badly to be inside her that it felt like a fresh wound.

"Shy…" he'd been about to apologize but didn't get the chance.

"Claim me Leto."

He stilled even as she writhed beneath him pressing her warm, satiny body against his as if the mere friction was addictive. When she reached between them and wrapped small fingers around his cock, he threw his head back and hissed at the sheer pleasure the simple touch brought forth. Shy didn't waste time. She guided the mushroomed tip of him to her saturated cunt and when he was properly aligned she begged, "Fuck me Leto. Please."

A low growl rumbled from his chest as he drove into her inch by glorious inch. She was so tight, wet, and hot that he knew in that moment that he'd found his heaven. He'd always second guessed Walker claiming but now he knew that angels were predestined. She was made for him alone and from this day forward neither of them would know the touch of another.

He pulled out almost all the way then drove home with greater force and began to rock his hips in a steady rhythm. His lips and teeth toured her body. He wanted to memorize every single inch of her and he wanted to do it tonight. Her taste, her scent, her sounds…as if on cue Shy gave a keening cry as her hips lifted to match his thrusts. Her pussy was so exquisite that he was fighting to keep from coming too soon, but he wanted to; he wanted to spill his seed so deep inside her that she'd be marked by him for all eternity.

Shy's legs lifted and wrapped around his waist forcing the long length of him deeper inside of her. She screamed and he quickened his pace, the wet sounds of their desire bouncing off the walls.

One strong hand gripped the halo around Shy's throat and while the other slide between their bodies to strum the pink pearl of her clit. Shy gasped and unlocked her ankles letting her feet drop back to the bed and spread her legs wider. "It's too much!"

He knew she was close. He could already feel the spasms in her channel as she tightened. He fucked her harder and faster while his relentless finger moved in faster, tighter circles. His lips found hers and he drew her lip into his mouth and sucked it even as she panted and fought to breathe. "Say it Shy."

She sounded panicked when she asked, "Say what?"

"Who do you belong to?"

When she didn't immediately respond he applied more pressure to her clit and stopped moving in circles to flick his finger rapidly up and down over the juicy nub, but stilled his dick inside her. Shy screamed and her body tightened wanting him to drive into her.

"*Who* do you belong to?" Leto demanded.

"YOU!" Shy cried. "I belong to you. I'm yours!"

She was rewarded with deep penetrating thrusts and that was all it took. "YOURS!" Shy shrieked as her body convulsed. Her pussy clamped down so tightly on his dick that Leto gave up all control and shot his release deep into her clenching channel even as it milked the warm jets from him. Finally, Shy was bound, *properly* marked, and finally claimed.

After long minutes when his cock finally emptied the last of his seed, Leto leaned over Shy, pulled her close to him and rolled until she sprawled naked across his chest with his dick still buried deep inside her. When she tried to wiggle free his hand clamped on her ass to hold her in place.

"Isn't it uncomfortable?" Vibrant blue eyes sought his in the dark.

Smiling, he brushed strands of red hair back from her face before kissing her forehead. "It is home. You are my home Shy and nothing ever has or ever will feel as right as being buried inside you. I want to stay here forever."

His heart melted when he saw her smile of satisfaction at his words.

"I love you Shy."

He watched her bite her lip as her brows furrowed. She didn't return his sentiment and he hadn't expected her to but he did feel sad that she felt obvious guilt over it. "You will grow to love me in time. I will prove my worth to you and our child."

"I-I trust you," she offered tremulously.

He smiled to himself. It was a start. Better than a start. She felt compelled to offer him something and her trust, as all Walkers knew, was a precursor to love. He was confident that he'd have her professing her love by dawn and his smile turned wicked at the challenge. "Get some sleep my Shy. I will need to fuck you again soon. A claiming is exhausting for a Walker's angel."

Shy pulled back from his chest to stare up at him, "Don't you need time to…recuperate?"

"No. I could take you again right now, and I want to, but I'm trying to be a considerate mate and you are already with child. I don't want to wear you out or harm our son."

Placing both hands on his thickly muscled chest, she pushed up until she was straddling him as he lay flat on his back under her. Wordlessly she began working her hips and when his hands clamped her thighs to still her, she lifted them to her breasts and moaned as she began to ride him faster.

Leto didn't like not being in control but the sheer bliss of his angel riding him was too exquisite for him to complain.

When Shy rode him to completion and collapsed spent on top of him he pulled from her and allowed her to rest. Swamped with exhaustion he too rested, but not long. He was determined to own not just her body but her heart before the dawning of a new day.

Chapter 28

"You're not going to Shy and Leto's wedding?" Conn asked already knowing the answer.

"No." York didn't look at his Commander as he continued to pummel the heavy bag hanging from a chain before him. Sweat dripped down his nose and his muscles bunched with each heavy blow that landed loudly.

"There are going to be unmated females York. It's as good a place as any to search for your angel."

York began punching the bag harder, his jaw muscle clenching. "I'm done looking!"

"You don't mean that."

"I do!" York stopped hitting the bag to frown at Conn. "It's not meant to be for all of us. Those of us who are meant to be alone need to accept our fate."

"You can't know that. Hell, just come to the reception and at least enjoy one of the bridesmaid's for a night."

"I don't want to enjoy a night!" York's expression faltered for a moment and Conn saw the pain and loneliness the other

Walker quickly masked. "I want *every* night. I want my angel and I want her now! I'm tired of waiting for it to happen." He jerked one fist out of his boxing glove then the other before dropping the worn gloves to the ground, "I'm done with it. From here on out, I'm resolving myself to being alone."

"Don't give up!"

"Easy for you to say," York's shoulders slumped as he turned away. "Do you have any idea how difficult it is watching you with Aries and your precious little Wynter? To want what you have and to know I'll never find it?"

Conn's eyes turned sad, "York, you just need to give it time. You've got to put yourself out there though. Come to the wedding," he implored.

Shaking his head as he stalked away York's lips thinned into a grim line. "I don't need to celebrate. I need to work."

Conn could only watch as his best friend and second-in-command disappeared into the locker room. He felt sorry for his friend and when his thoughts flashed to his angel and their daughter, his heart swelled with so much love and appreciation for what he had that tears stung his eyes. He couldn't imagine his life without Aries and he could understand where York's agony stemmed from.

Unlike most Walkers, the Celtic sentry sought out his angel. He actually looked forward to being afflicted and was hopeful every time his eyes locked on those of an unmated woman that she would be his one.

Looking to his side, Conn punched the still swinging heavy bag in frustration. He could—and had on several occasions--killed to defend his friend, he could maim another if they ever challenged York's character, hell he could even slap York himself when he took too many chances with his own life but this…" Conn heaved a great sigh knowing that he could do nothing to mend his friend's broken heart and worse he couldn't even make the hollow promise of an angel waiting somewhere in his friend's future.

Walker mates were rare and extremely hard to find. While unmated Walker men often enjoyed the pleasure of women, the one-night stands had yet to produce any viable mate or legitimate angel.

"Did you find York?"

Aries' soft words had Conn turning to smile warmly at his angel.

"Yes," he reached out and pulled his dark haired mate into his arms. "He's upset and I can't fix it and it's killing me."

Aries smiled up at him, "Don't feel guilty, I'm sure he'll find what he's looking for soon." Delicate brows speared down before shooting up over rounded eyes, "I have a friend from when I used to live here. I could look her up. You know, set York up on a date?"

Conn dipped his head to brush his lips over Aries'. "Thank you for the offer but I'd hate to subject him to another rejection. I don't think he could take it right now."

"Well, what can we do?"

Drawing in a deep breath, Conn felt another bout of guilt assail him at his angel's expectant look. "Nothing beautiful. There isn't anything we can do for him. This is one battle our friend must endure alone."

Aries' lips pursed in a moue of disappointment. "Well maybe Leto and Shy won't work out."

A deep chuckle vibrated from Conn's chest, "I thought you liked Shy."

"I do," she shrugged negligently, "but I like York more."

"Careful beautiful," he gripped her chin with his finger to hold her in place. "No declarations of admiration for my second-in-command. It brings out my need for dominance."

Aries smiled wickedly, "Good Commander, are you implying that you think you've got what it takes to dominate me?"

"I *know* I do."

She jerked her chin free and pulled from his embrace as she sauntered to the door making sure to give her hips a little extra swing as she walked before turning and winking at her Walker. "Well, there's only one way to find out. Isn't there?"

Conn dipped his head and followed his angel out of the room knowing with all certainty that if she ever asked he'd gladly follow her into the burning fires of hell.

***

TWO WEEKS AFTER THE BIRTH OF LYON REIGNS

"What's up," York queried as he stalked into the conference room. Flanked by his own team of three mercenaries, he ignored the other four Walkers relaxing in chairs or lining the wall as he walked directly up to Conn.

Conn's brows drew together in a deep frown. "I thought you and your men were taking Mason's mission?"

"Let him find his own damn sister," York growled.

Conn's frown softened. "Shy's been claimed York." He lowered his voice, "You can't have her."

"I know." The words were bit out on a snarl. "But Monroe said your mission is a special request from her. I'd like to know what it is."

Conn nodded sharply and stood taller as York turned and took a place next to his men standing against one wall.

"As you all are aware," Conn addressed the room, "Shy Brookes has been claimed by Leto Reigns. That makes her one of us. While being held at the Megalya facility Shy's family was told that she'd taken a special assignment in the Philippines." The corner of Conn's mouth tweaked. "Problem is Shy apparently has a sister that's just as stubborn as she is.

Her sister traveled to the Philippines to locate Shy and bring her home. Shy's sister left the States four months ago and no one's heard from her since."

Conn turned and began pacing. "While Shy and her son Lyon are protected under Walker rule, Shy's sister is not. She is not a Walker, nor has she been claimed by one." He turned to narrow his eyes on York. "Shy is asking for our help. The mission is voluntary." Conn began pacing again, "Leto can't go. He won't leave Shy and Lyon right now and I don't blame him. Likewise, Aries has asked me to remain here with her and Wynter and I will, which means…" He didn't get to finish.

"I'll go." York pushed off the wall.

"Don't you want to discuss it with your men first?" Conn frowned.

"I didn't say my men and I would go," York uncrossed his arms that had been strapped across his thick chest. "I said *I* would go."

Conn shrugged as he turned, “Fine, follow me. I’ll brief you fully.”

The two men were halfway to the door when Marko shoved off the wall, “You need backup?”

York stopped and smiled over his shoulder. “It’s one woman. I don’t suspect I’ll need assistance. You and the boys get back to Apex. You’re in charge of Mason’s mission. I’ll be back in two weeks.”

Marko smiled from under the dark wisp of black bangs that hung into his eyes and turned to punch Lok in the shoulder, “You heard the man. Let’s roll.”

***

Shy paced in front of the large bay window that looked out at the heavily forested grounds of StoneCrow estates. She wrung her hands and chewed on her bottom lip before asking for the hundredth time, “Do you think she’s okay?”

Leto, clad in only a pair of dark sweat pants, set little Lyon’s tightly wrapped sleeping form into his crib before smiling sensually and padding in bare feet to his angel. He wrapped his powerful arms around her and pulled her into his chest all while being amazed at the sheer rightness of having her near. “She’ll be fine my Shy. They’ll find her.”

“They?” Shy protested. “Aries said only York went. What if he’s not enough? What if he can’t find her? What if he gets hurt?”

Leto had to bite back the jealous retort at her concern over York’s welfare. After he’d claimed Shy, York had backed off and Leto had to respect him for that; not to mention that the man had volunteered to retrieve Shy’s sister from some place in the Philippines. Yet it didn’t mean he would ever permit the Walker near his angel after he’d expressed his desire to have her. If anything, York’s actions now pronounced the Celtic Walker’s belief or hope that he still had a chance with Shy. The thought was enraging!

“York will find her,” it was difficult for Leto to force the words out. “He’s…*good* at what he does.”

Shy spun in his arms to face him, tears flooding her eyes. “But what if something’s happened. What if he can’t find her?”

Leto pulled her close and rested his chin on atop her head as he spoke, "If he fails my Shy, then I will go and I swear to you I will not return without your sister."

She sighed and melted into his embrace. It felt like home and offered some solace against the storm of worry and fear that the Megalya had somehow gotten their hands on her sister.

Leto squeezed her tighter then pulled back and focused over her head on the wall. She recognized the action. He was getting a telepathic communication from another Walker through the mist.

Once bound and claimed, Shy too had learned to communicate through the mist but unlike Walkers who were able to communicate with *all* other Walkers, Shy could only communicate with her mate.

Leto blinked then smiled down at Shy. "Your parents have just arrived."

For the first time since the birth of their son, Lyon, Shy felt hope blossom. Monroe, finally satisfied that Shy's family was no longer under surveillance by the Megalya, had granted permission for them to be escorted to the estate. It would be the first time Shy would see them since she'd left for her internship nearly nine months earlier.

Jenny had been right, Shy's pregnancy was rapid and surprisingly Shy was grateful for it. It was the perfect excuse to tell her parents. She'd convinced them that she'd fallen madly in love and that she and Leto, who she said was a fellow student, had eloped. The timing was perfect for her to lie and say that she'd gotten pregnant right away.

Leto beamed down at his wife and grabbed a hand leading her to their son.

Wrapped in a royal blue, fuzzy, baby blanket, Lyon was lifted from his crib and Shy's heart squeezed—as it always did—at the sight of her Walker husband holding their child. She didn't think it was possible for one heart to hold so much happiness.

Smiling at his angel, Leto pulled Shy into his embrace and lowered Lyon so that Shy could pull down the blanket under the baby's chin and peck a kiss to impossibly small lips. He could scent her happiness and it only served to encourage his own.

In the Megalya labs he'd vowed to spend his life hunting and killing Walker enemies but Shy had pulled him from his plans of a tortured existence and with the remarkable gift of their son she'd well and truly saved him.

Shy looked up in time to catch the familiar scowl that marred her mate's handsome features. She couldn't help the smile that crooked her lips. "What is it?" She already knew. Leto always got serious and frowned every time he was about to profess his undying love and loyalty.

"I love you my Shy. Do you know I'd do anything in the world for you and the son you've given me? I would die for you both."

"Yes my love," her lips spread in a grin. She tiptoed and Leto bent to meet her lips as she kissed him then kept her lips pressed to his and whispered, "and I love you for it….*we* love you for it." She pulled back and smiled wickedly, "Now let's put your vow to the test and go and introduce you to my father."

Leto growled low in his chest, "I do not fear your father."

Shy laughed and turned toward the door, "You shouldn't. Mom's the one that you gotta watch out for." When Leto's face blanked she laughed harder, "Come on *my* Leto and stop worrying. If I love you, they'll love you and I love you more than I can stand."

Exclusive Excerpt

Hunted

by

Susan A. Bliler

Trudging through the thick brush, Sia barely noticed when her rifle slipped from her left hand and landed with a heavy thud in the tall wet grass. Annoyance bunched her brows together over her thin nose as she glared down at her weapon. *What the fuck?*

Bending to pick up the rifle, she was too slow. Andre, who'd been pulling up the rear, reached down and snatched it out from under her cold wet fingers. He stood and held the weapon out to her while shaking his head, derision curling his lip.

Annoyed more that Andre had witnessed her folly than at herself for actually committing it, Sia reached up and grabbed her rifle, all the while glowering up at the much taller Andre.

With her hand on her rifle, Sia made to pull the rifle to her, but Andre held strong.

"Hey!" Sia yelled trying to draw Andre's eyes up from where they were focused, but his eyes didn't move. Sia looked down to see what was so damn important that Andre refused to release her rifle. Shock washed over her as she realized that Andre was staring at her left hand as it gripped her rifle. Her small knuckles were coated in blood and dripping crimson droplets down the length of her barrel. Sia's eyes traced up her arm and she reached over with her right hand to finger the fabric of her sleeve at her left shoulder where a hole gaped open. She pulled the hole open revealing a wound. She'd been shot. She looked up at Andre, her expression confused.

"COLBY!" Andre shouted for the medic. Andre yanked the rifle from Sia's grip and leaned it against the nearest tree before he dropped his pack and set his rifle on top. Standing he reached up and pulled both arm loops of Sia's pack off her shoulders.

"I got it!" Sia barked at Andre annoyed. Andre dropped her pack next to his and reached up to quickly unbutton the front of her camo shirt as Colby stepped through the brush.

"What's up? Who's hurt?" Colby questioned as he tried to catch his breath.

"She's been shot." Andre answered in a thick Russian accent, without taking his eyes off his task.

Colby's eyes flashed to Sia, "What…When?"

As Andre unfastened the last button, he opened Sia's shirt and pushed it off her shoulders. Blood stained the form fitting green tank top she wore underneath.

"Last firefight." Andre answered.

Sia pulled away from Andre, trying to pull her shirt back on, "Jesus Christ, it's just a flesh wound. I didn't even feel it."

Colby grabbed her elbow and spun her to him, "Whoa, let me look at that." Colby leaned in and inspected her wound, "Shit! That's more than just a flesh wound." Colby looked up at the much taller Andre, "This is gonna take a minute."

Nodding Andre grabbed his rifle and disappeared through the foliage. Sia heard a faint, "Set up a perimeter, Sia needs medical attention."

"Jesus, Colby! Can't you just bandage it up? We can't get caught out here." Sia plopped down on the fallen log that Colby led her to. Colby straddled the log as he pulled off his pack and unzipped it. He pulled out a bottle of antiseptic and poured it on Sia's wound causing her to inhale in a long hiss of pain.

"Bullet went clean through, but we'll need to stop the bleeding." Colby doused her arm again with a second slosh of antiseptic.

Andre returned, rifle at the ready when Colby looked up at him. Colby's serious look halted Andre and Sia watched as Colby looked at Andre then glanced her way and inclined his head at the same time.

Whoa, what's going on?

Whatever it was Andre understood. Andre used his boot to clear a spot on the forest floor before he left and returned with an armload of kindling.

"No way!" Sia jumped up and was pulling her shirt on when Colby grabbed her arm.

"Sia, we've gotta get it closed." Colby pleaded. "You're losing too much blood and there's no other way."

Andre never stopped his work, he was now on his hands and knees with his flint, sending showers of sparks raining down on the kindling.

Angrily, Sia reached down and grabbed Colby's pack, shoving it into his chest, "Put some fucking gauze in it and let's get rolling, it'll be night soon."

Colby grabbed the pack and looked at Sia apologetically through his thin wire framed glasses, "I'm sorry… this is gonna hurt."

Sia was grabbed from behind by Andre who easily wrestled her to the ground. "Are you fucking kidding me? Get the fuck off me!"

Andre wrapped an arm around her throat in a half rear-naked choke while his other pinned her right arm in place. His legs were wrapped around her hips and crossed at the ankle over her knees. Andre held Sia in place as he rolled slightly to his right, exposing his hunting knife to Colby.

About the Author

I'm a Paralegal by profession and when I'm not working or volunteering I'm writing.

I am one of six children and I am blessed to have a twin sister. She and I work for the same agency, in the same office, and are inseparable…my poor husband! I'm married and have a step-son who adores my sister. We also have two dogs, one black lab and one yellow, (Zena and Jimmy) I did NOT name the dogs.

I'm a huge fan of MMA, boxing, hockey, 30 Seconds to Mars, the Killers, and DMX. I also love to read because it encourages me to write. (I always hate it when authors add that they love coffee and chocolate. Really? Who doesn't love coffee and chocolate.) Anyway, I love beer…kidding. I don't love beer but we are engaged in a very serious relationship. (Mom, please don't call me when you read this.)

Please visit me at SusanBliler.com for exclusive excerpts of soon to be released works. Also, please leave feedback. Believe it or not I actually read your opinions/suggestions and try to adapt my work accordingly.

ps: I have the best fans in the world! Keep e-mailing and leaving comments on my site and check back for soon to be implemented free reads and book give aways and stay tuned there are more Skin Walkers to come!

Made in the USA
Lexington, KY
25 April 2014